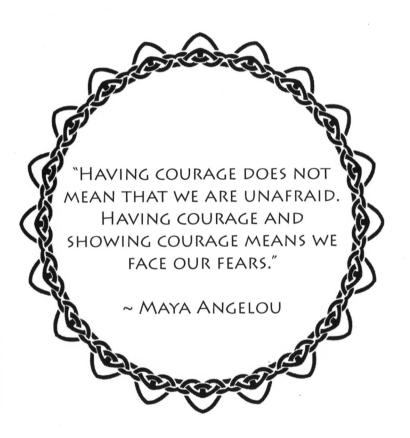

"HAVING COURAGE DOES NOT
MEAN THAT WE ARE UNAFRAID.
HAVING COURAGE AND
SHOWING COURAGE MEANS WE
FACE OUR FEARS."

~ MAYA ANGELOU

TO TED, HENRY & FLORA:
MAY YOU ALWAYS FIND THE COURAGE TO
FACE YOUR FEARS AND FORGE YOUR OWN PATH

First published in Great Britain in 2018
Hayes Creative Publishing, 136 Ermine St, Cambridge, CB23 3PQ, England

ISBN 978-1-9993049-0-4

Celtic knot line art = designed by GDJ on OpenClipArt.org
Tribal boundaries = based on maps by Chris Rudd
Cover photo = taken by Maxim Zorin for CreativeMarket.com

CARASSOUNA

COMING HOME

JEN HAYES

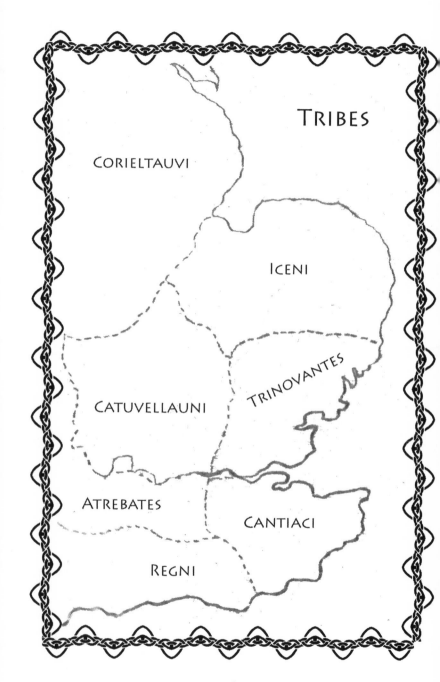

TRIBES

CORIELTAUVI

ICENI

CATUVELLAUNI

TRINOVANTES

ATREBATES

CANTIACI

REGNI

CORIELTAUVI

THORNHAM

HUNSTANTON

WARHAM

ICENI

CAISTOR
ST EDMUND

THETFORD

BURGH

TRINOVANTES

CATUVELLAUNI

PLACES

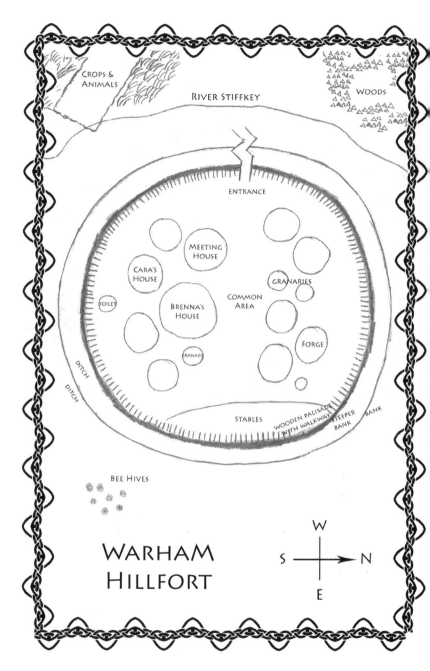

CROPS & ANIMALS

RIVER STIFFKEY

WOODS

ENTRANCE

MEETING HOUSE

CARA'S HOUSE

TOILET

BRENNA'S HOUSE

COMMON AREA

GRANARIES

GRANARY

FORGE

DITCH

DITCH

STABLES

WOODEN PALISADE WITH WALKWAY

STEEPER BANK

BANK

BANK

BEE HIVES

WARHAM HILLFORT

W

S — N

E

PEOPLE

CARASSOUNA = ME

BELLATOR = MY FATHER

ALAUNA = MY MOTHER

LUCILIA & MATO = MY SISTER & BROTHER

BRENNA = OUR CHIEF

SOLINUS & ILLICA = MY FOSTER PARENTS

DRUSTAN & SENNI = MY BEST FRIENDS

MORNA = MY HORSE

VASTINI = MY ARCH-ENEMY

GAVO = MY INTENDED FUTURE HUSBAND

THERE ARE OTHERS, WHOM I WILL
INTRODUCE TO YOU INSIDE...

ONE

I was eight winters when I left home. Not old enough to know where I was going, but old enough to know why. The bittersweet scent of thyme upon the fire still reminds me of that day.

I can smell the thyme now, even before we're in sight of the hillfort. The fires burn constantly inside the round-houses, providing heat and light, and I think I see a faint wisp of smoke rising in the still and sticky summer air.

'Almost there now,' calls my foster father from a short way behind me as he stops briefly at the river to let his horse drink; this river I know so well, every bend and every tree now reminding me of my childhood adventures.

Sent out to gather firewood or forage for herbs and berries, we would cool down from the summer heat in the clear, fresh water. I remember the sounds of splashing and laughing – our only worry whether our mams would think we were gone too long and come looking for us.

Now, four winters later, I'm almost back home. Who am I now? Who will they all be? I have no idea what to expect, and feel my stomach tighten into knots.

I pull back on Morna for her to stop and wait for Solinus to catch up.

'You feeling a bit shook up?' he asks.

I nod – I guess the look on my face gives away my feelings; I was never any good at hiding them.

'Don't worry now,' he says. 'They're all expecting you – word was sent from the Wighton clan just yesterday when we stopped for the night. A clan member coming home is always a big deal. That sweet smoke can only mean one thing: a feast. And I'm certainly ready for that!' he adds, laughing.

I give him a nervous smile and we continue on, giving a click for our horses to keep following the river.

It's not unusual, my story. All children are sent off for fosterage – that's just the way it is. We leave home when we've lived eight winters, collected by our foster parents – often people we've never met before. We travel to their homes and live with them for four winters, continuing our training there. Children of warriors, children of blacksmiths, children of craftspeople – we all do the same. The clan chiefs make the fosterage arrangements, although sometimes parents have a say. Never the children. We are sent for a greater purpose: the well-being of our clan.

But my placement was to help more than just my clan; it was for my tribe, the Iceni, to help seal our alliance with the Trinovantes. We are a powerful people, but there are still those we fear. My father says we need this alliance to build our strength, to stand up to the Catuvellauni should we need to. Change is coming; everyone knows it.

We come to a fork in the path and leave the riverside, heading up the hill. Riding through overgrown brambles, just over the rise, I spot the hillfort. I am home.

After so long, I expect it to look different, for things to have changed. But it's just as I remember – the towering wooden palisades standing guard; the smoke rising into the deep blue sky beyond. A steep bank topped with palisades forms an inner ring to protect the houses. Around this, a deep ditch is dug into the earth, surrounded by another steep, grassy bank. A formidable sight, and a closely guarded home. At the mouth of the fort, a single opening – sealed off by two gigantic wooden doors and flanked by tall, guarded towers. These are further protected by earthen ramparts to waylay any would-be attackers.

'What do you think?' Solinus asks, tilting his head to the hillfort.

The truth is, I don't know. It feels wonderful to be home and tremendously scary all at once.

Nothing to do but face it head on.

'I'm ready,' I say. Tapping my heels to Morna's side

with a 'tsk, tsk,' we ride towards the gate.

As we approach, a guard shouts down from one of the watchtowers. 'State your name and business,' he demands.

'I am Cara,' I call to him, trying to be brave. 'Carassouna Vendi, returning home from fosterage.'

A surprised reply comes back, 'Cara, I didn't even recognise you!' The guard disappears from the window, then a moment later we hear the thumps of bars being removed and one of the huge double gates swings open.

The guard hurries out. I can see he is young, not much older than I am. He walks quickly towards us, relaxed and welcoming now, and holds out his arms.

'We've been expecting you,' he says. 'You're so tall now! Your mam and tad will be so happy to see you. Do you remember me?'

I shake my head.

'Luccus. Second cousin on your tad's side,' he says.

A dim recognition flickers in the corner of my brain… this is going to be more difficult than I thought if I can't even recognise my own family...

Then something catches my eye – two figures coming towards me across the side of the hill, where the downstream river and woods lie further beyond. Now these people look more familiar; the ones I've been waiting for and dreaming of – my best friends.

Sliding down from my horse, I take the reins in my hand and stroke the side of her neck. My beloved Morna, my constant companion, my only connection with home those long seasons away. 'There now, girl, look who it is,' I whisper to her.

'Cara, is it you?' I hear Drustan's voice call. The same as before, only different now – deeper, stronger.

I wave and the figures break into a run as I turn and lay the reins across Morna's back with a pat.

'Stay here, girl,' I say to her and start walking towards my friends.

Drustan reaches me first, his eyes shining above his huge smile. His hair gleams golden in the late afternoon sun and I can't help but notice how his face has changed. He is much taller too, and his arms surround me in a giant hug. We both laugh, and I feel at once relieved and reassured.

Senni has hung back a bit, giving us space, but now we reach our arms out to each other and it's like we've never been apart.

'Senni,' I say, now the tears filling my eyes; my throat choked with the effort to hold them back.

I pull away and hold her at arm's length. Her fiery hair, as red as ever, hangs down to her waist, beautifully braided with beads. Her pale skin is still rosy from running.

She laughs and says, 'Cara, you're so tall now! How are you? How was your journey? Are you tired? Is Morna still eating all the apples?'

Trust Senni to make me feel like nothing has changed!

I'm so happy, I give her another huge hug and breathe a sigh of relief.

Maybe everything is going to be okay after all.

'You wouldn't believe how nervous I've been,' I say. 'Oh wait, I need to introduce you.'

I lead them over to where Solinus waits with Luccus and the horses.

'This is Solinus, my foster father,' I say to them. Then to Solinus, 'And these are my oldest, dearest friends. Senni and Drustan,' I add, gesturing towards them.

'Pleasure,' he replies. 'Our Cara is going to be missed a great deal. I'm trusting you to take good care of her.'

'Yes, sir,' says Drustan.

'More likely, I'll take good care of them, Solinus,' I say, and he laughs heartily.

'I know you will,' he says.

We stand there, soaking in the warming rays of the late afternoon sun and chatting about our journey. Solinus is so good-natured, he gets on easily with my friends and cousin, and I consider the colliding of my two worlds – fosterage and birth, families and friends, they all come together here.

After a little while, Morna tosses her head and gives a gentle whinny. We all turn to look at her, surprised.

'I think she's trying to tell us something…', I say.

'Like she's hungry!' adds Senni jokingly, which makes everyone laugh.

I stroke Morna's neck, but feel reluctant to break the spell of this perfect reunion. Solinus does instead.

'Shall we go?' he asks.

Drustan takes the reins of both horses and my cousin leads us through the gates, waving to the other guard in the watchtower.

Nothing smells and looks quite like home. It's just as I remembered, the bustling activity of our daily clan life. My foster clan was much smaller, much quieter. I've so missed this noise and sense of motion, of something always happening.

Drustan is watching me and says, 'I missed it too.'

'It's a bit quieter where we are,' says my foster father, 'a smaller clan.' He looks around and then settles back on me. 'It will be even quieter now,' he says wistfully and puts his arm around me.

I hug him back and start to feel a sense of loss – I'm going to miss this kind, gentle man who's been my father for the past four winters. Although he could never replace my real father, he has loved me as his own daughter and cared for me. I've been so nervous about coming home that I've spent the entire journey going through different scenarios in my mind. Now I remember what I'll be losing and wrap my arms more tightly around him, then pull away and wipe my eyes briskly with the back of my hand. Solinus rubs my shoulder and gives me a quick kiss on the head.

'You'll get back into things soon enough,' says Drustan.

'It didn't take me too long,' Senni adds with a smile.

Then I hear a booming call, 'CARA!'

My father, Bellator – the clan's lead warrior – strides towards me from behind one of the roundhouses.

'Father!' I call and run towards him, so happy to see him well, healthy and in the flesh after all this time. My worries and fears vanish as he sweeps me up into his arms and twirls me around like he did when I was a little girl. I laugh and cry, my face buried in his shoulder, his strong arms making me feel safe and secure.

'Oh my sweet Cara, I'm so happy you're home,' he says, his voice muffled in my hair. He sets me down gently, tears flowing down his cheeks but with no concern for showing his emotion. 'We got word it would be today... and here you are. You're really here.' He laughs, pinches his nose, rubs his eyes, and sniffs.

My cheeks are wet with salty tears, and I also laugh and wipe them away.

My father moves forward to shake my foster father's hand. 'Solinus. Thank you for taking such good care of my little girl.'

'She's not so little anymore,' Solinus replies.

'No, I can see that,' my father says a bit wistfully, but he recovers quickly and asks, 'Good travels here? Any... problems?' he asks cryptically, setting me on edge. What is he talking about? Me? Something else? Someone else?

'None too challenging, Bellator,' Solinus grins, glancing at me out of the corner of his eye. He pauses and lowers his voice slightly. 'Although Thetford is much on edge, they think it could be soon.' We passed through Thetford, the tribal centre of the Iceni, on our journey and stopped for two nights to rest and replenish supplies. Now I wonder if there were other reasons we stayed so long…

'Well, they're always worried,' my father replies. 'If you were that close to the border, you'd always be worried too. I can see why though – if the Catuvellauni do decide to attack, that will be the first place they hit.'

My father's brow briefly creases with concern, but then he looks down at me and relaxes.

'That's enough fighting talk for now,' he says, 'you both must be starving – and your horses too. Let's get them bedded down, and Cara – we must bring you to your mam. Senni, Drustan – can you please see to the horses?'

'Of course,' Senni replies and Drustan nods.

I walk back over to Morna and stroke her neck. 'Good girl,' I say to her. 'I'll come visit you later.'

Her big, brown eyes look deep into mine. I think she realises we're home as well, and I rest my forehead briefly on the bridge of her nose before giving her one more pat.

'We'll see you later,' Drustan says to me and leads Morna away while Senni takes Solinus' horse. They guide the horses back out of the hillfort, headed in the direction of the paddocks where they can graze before being settled down in the stables. I know they'll treat the horses to some flax leaves to help them recover from the long journey, and maybe even some crab apples which are just coming into season.

My father walks us across the common area, and everyone we pass waves and calls out a greeting to me. It's a bit overwhelming, but also nice – I feel quite special.

We walk around the meeting house and pass by the entrance to the largest – and most luxurious – roundhouse in the hillfort: our chief's home. Brenna, the chief of our clan, is both a good friend of my father's and a formidable leader. Her presence makes me feel a bit on edge and I wonder if she's home; glancing through the doorway, I can see heavy woven curtains and iron fire guards in the shape of horses, but no one moving about.

'Home at last,' my father says as we arrive at the doorway to our house. As the clan's top warrior – and Brenna's most trusted confidante – my father has the house closest to her. It's an honour, and for me also a source of some anxiety as it means I often feel observed.

All of these old feelings rush back as he steps aside to let me go first. I walk in hesitantly, my eyes adjusting to the dim light inside. I see two figures on the floor playing with what looks like wooden dolls. I hear a dull thud and look up to see my mother standing there, the iron pot she was holding now on the floor.

'My Cara!' my mother cries as she runs towards me, arms outstretched. She grabs me and pulls me close to her. 'Welcome home, my child!' she says as she holds me tight, as though she'll never let go.

I hug her, and let her hug me, but then pull back a bit – 'I'm not a child any more,' I remind her.

'No. No, of course not,' she says reluctantly. 'Although you'll always be my child,' she says with a smile and touches my cheek fondly.

'Look, little ones – your sister is here!' Mam cries.

The two children on the floor stand up and come over uncertainly. I think I recognise the girl as my sister Lucilia, but she was little more than a baby when I left. The boy I have never seen.

'You remember Lucilia surely,' says my mam, touching the girl on the shoulder. 'Much taller than when you left, and seven winters already. And this is Mato.' She ruffles the hair of the little boy. 'Just three now,' she adds, then bends down to give him a quick kiss on the cheek.

He shows me a tentative smile then ducks behind mam, hiding in the folds of her peplum – our summery, sleeveless, woollen dresses.

Lucilia slowly comes closer and gives me a little hug. 'I've missed you,' she says.

I immediately feel guilty – I'm not sure I've missed her. I've been practically the only child of Solinus and his wife, Illica, while in fosterage. Their children had already grown and started their own families, some moving away and others with their own roundhouses. I had gotten used to all of the attention, but I find myself saying 'me too' and giving her a hug. No sense in making her sad when we weren't even going to be together much longer – she'll be going away for her fosterage soon.

'Run along now little ones, and feed the chickens,' Mam says to them. 'There's much to be done before the feast.' Then to me, 'Cara, you'll be in charge of the bread and the ornaments.'

'Alauna,' my father says, 'she hasn't even set her bag down yet. Let's give her some time to rest before she has to meet with the rest of the tribe.'

'Well,' my mother replies, 'I think there's nothing like work to make you feel right at home…but if you insist, I'll do it instead,' she finishes and winks at me.

'And of course, hello Solinus,' she says to my foster father. 'So happy the journey went to plan. You have much to tell us of the past few years,' she says meaningfully.

'There's plenty of time for that later,' says my father, taking down four mugs and filling them with honey mead from an old earthenware jug.

We raise them and toast.

'To Cara,' my father says. 'Our beloved eldest daughter – once a child, now a young woman. And our future chief.'

TWO

A little while later, after I'd unpacked my bag and Mam had shown me where everything is now (most of it familiar, but many things forgotten and some in new places), I pull out my best peplum and cloak. I feel a bit shaky thinking about the gathering ahead. This is the first time I've seen everyone since I was a child. What will they expect of me?

I dress quickly then carefully put on the ornaments of our warrior noble class – a golden torc around my neck, bracelets and armband. It's all very heavy, and I feel the cool weight against my skin.

I check my hair in the bronzed mirror. Almost waist-length now, my light blonde hair looks white against my skin – just as Morna's mane and tail appear white against her dapple-grey coat. I suddenly wonder what she's doing now, and quickly pull a few strands from each side back into a clasp. There, that will do. It's important I look my best tonight, but I feel much better freshly bathed and dressed after so many dusty, dirty days of travel.

I leave my mam sweeping the roundhouse floor.

'Don't be long,' she calls after me, 'we'll be gathering soon.'

I head back out of the hillfort towards the nearest paddock and see Morna munching happily. She trots over to me and I stroke her forehead. It's so funny with her – sometimes when I'm riding her, I feel so close to her it's as if we can read each other's minds. Other times, she's definitely just a horse!

I laugh out loud and a voice behind me calls, 'What's so funny then?'

I turn and see Drustan approaching, a basket of grain in his arms.

'Oh nothing, just thinking about Morna,' I say.

He smiles and comes next to me, setting the basket down between us as Morna noses into it. 'You two are just like each other…but I think she eats a bit more,' he says and we both laugh. 'So tell me more about your time away. What was your family like?'

'Oh, Solinus and Illica were more amazing than I ever dreamed possible – I couldn't have asked for a better foster family. Their children are all grown now, so I had lots of space in their house and so much attention from them. What about yours?' I ask him.

Suddenly his smile drops. 'Well, let's just say I missed my parents,' he says, looking down.

'Oh,' I reply, worriedly. 'Not good then?'

'No,' he looks at me very seriously, 'not great…but it's not to get into now – today is your day.'

We stand in silence for a few moments, and I'm not sure if I should push him to talk about it. I know our time is short, so I'll leave it for another day.

'It's funny,' I say to him, 'I've been waiting for this day for so long, I almost can't believe it's finally here.'

He punches my arm jokingly. 'You kept us waiting long enough!' he says.

'It's not my fault you're so much older than me and yet I'm so much better than you are,' I retort.

'Better?!' he says, a mischievous look on his face.

'Just you wait and see, Morna and I will ride circles around the rest of you,' I say with a smile.

'Hhmph,' he says, but I can see a small smile on his face. 'That I look forward to seeing.'

He gives Morna a pat to get her out of the grain.

'That's enough for you, girl, let's save some for the others,' he says then turns to look at me, leaning against the paddock wall.

He obviously doesn't want to talk about his fosterage right now, so I digress to the Lughnasa festival I've just spent with the Trinovantes. It's such an important time of year, the beginning of the harvest, that we celebrate with feasting, dancing, games and competitions. Each tribe does it a little differently, with clans also having their own customs and traditions. But everywhere it's a time of great celebration – with long summer days and plenty of food for everyone to eat.

Drustan listens, nodding and smiling once in a while. As I go on though, his eyes seem to sadden. 'It sounds like you had a great time there', he says finally.

I shift awkwardly, wondering if I've played it up too much.

'But what of the alliance?' he blurts out, turning abruptly to rest his arms on top of the paddock wall with a deep sigh. So that's what it is.

I turn and rest my arms next to his, my bracelets jingling lightly. I look up and follow his gaze across the paddock and over the hills, shimmering golden-green in the late afternoon sun.

'Well…' I begin slowly. It was no secret the reason behind my placement with the Trinovantes; people who knew were quite open about it, although there was never a big announcement. But still I pause, not sure how to continue.

'Sorry to interrupt you two,' my father's deep voice breaks the silence. Drustan and I both straighten up quickly and turn around, leaving the conversation. 'We're almost ready to start, and Carassouna is needed. Drustan, please go ahead into the meeting house – we'll follow shortly.'

'Of course, Bellator,' Drustan says. He gives me a serious look and nods, then walks off.

Now Tad looks at me, and I can see the love and care in his eyes. 'Cara, you must know how proud I am of you. Solinus has told me of your achievements with the Burgh clan, and this bodes well for your future. Brenna has also been informed and wishes to meet with you alone soon. She'll be there tonight, of course, and will be watching to see how you respond to the full clan gathering.'

'Of course, father,' I say. 'What will they expect me to do?'

My tad laughs, 'Now don't worry - it's nothing too serious tonight. You're still a warrior in training, everyone knows that. Twelve is too young to take on a full role.'

'But, I don't know...' I begin.

He cuts me off quickly, 'You are doing well. No one would expect you to be ready yet.'

Now he looks apologetic and kisses my forehead. 'You look lovely, my sweet Cara,' he says and smiles at me.

I wish I could stay here forever, basking in the glow of the afternoon sunshine and my tad's love, Morna by my side. I don't feel ready to take on these responsibilities – I don't even know if I want them. More than anything, I want to travel, to explore – to ride off on Morna, the wind in my hair, the sun on my back. If fostering far away showed me anything, it was how vast and beautiful our land is, and how much more there is to see. It's dangerous to travel too far inland; it's dangerous to set out to sea. But danger is what makes it so exciting: to explore the unknown.

Deep in thought, Tad guides me towards the meeting house and the gathering – my gathering.

As we approach, I hear the buzz of excited conversation, distinct voices rising in passion every now and then. There are streams of smoke weaving through the roof – the fire must just have been stoked – and the perfumed scent of thyme fills the thick, warm air.

We stop just before the doorway and I adjust my ornaments, brush back the stray hairs against my face and stand up straight, then nod to my father.

'I'm ready,' I say.

He nods and walks into the meeting house. Instantly, the gathered crowd quieten and I can hear him move purposefully to somewhere near the centre.

'Well met!' he says loudly. 'My daughter Carassouna has recently celebrated her twelfth winter, and as is tradition, she has been returned from fosterage. Her foster parents, Illica and Solinus have looked after her safely these four long winters, and I am honoured to have Solinus with us here today.'

The crowd claps enthusiastically.

'Now,' he continues, 'most of you will have heard the plans for Carassouna – that when three more winters have passed, she will be married to Gavo, son of Totia and Brigio.'

A few murmured voices rise from the hushed silence. Most of the hillfort would have known this already, but those who haven't heard are probably feeling a bit shocked at this news.

Totia and Brigio are elite members of the Trinovantes tribe. As one of the northern strongholds, our clan is responsible for securing the boundaries of the Iceni tribal land; but with Brenna as our chief, we are also considered a key diplomatic clan.

My marriage will help seal the alliance between the Trinovantes and Iceni tribes. If the Catuvellauni continue trying to grow their power, wealth and influence, this alliance will be essential to keep them at bay. Our land, our homes, our animals – even our people – are at risk.

Having spent these four winters with the Trinovantes, their plan has already begun to work – I now feel an incredible loyalty to both tribes.

My father continues, 'Brigio is a warrior of much renown and significant wealth; this alliance will mean a lasting peace and partnership. Carassouna and Gavo will return to live here and complete their training...until Cara can take over as chief when the time comes.'

As he finishes this sentence, a great roar of voices erupts, everyone asking questions at once.

'But why should we prepare for Brenna's successor?'

'What aren't you telling us, Bellator?'

'Surely you don't expect us to allow such a young woman to lead our entire clan?'

I feel my knees weaken at the rush of anger and passion in their voices, but their words make me feel bold, defiant.

Tad keeps his cool and calmly replies, 'Now, now everyone, this is all to be discussed still in tribunal – let's not forget why we are here today!' He laughs lightly. 'But we have no secrets here. Secrets pull us apart; communication keeps us together. There is still much debating and discussion to come. But on this day – let us celebrate. It is a joyous occasion, as my eldest daughter returns!'

And with that grand statement, I take my cue and sweep through the huge wicker doors into the meeting house, walking towards the fire whilst the roundhouse erupts in clapping and cheers. As my eyes adjust to the dim light, I can see the benches tightly packed with the most important and powerful adults in the clan, the space beyond filled with children, teens and the rest of the group.

Many faces look familiar; many more do not. So many changes can happen in the space of a fosterage. I had never realised our clan was so large, but then I had never stood before them in such a way, previously relegated to the outer ring as a child. There are at least ninety people –

probably a hundred – and all are watching me.

The fire in the centre of the house burns brightly, lighting the faces of those closest and throwing shadows deep into the recesses of the roundhouse. The largest iron cauldron is hanging still over the fire, with other pots pulled off to the side, while fresh bread stays warm nearby.

I smile and look around, overwhelmed but also happy to be home. I see Senni standing near the back and she gives me a little wave. Near her is Drustan, and on the other side of him my little brother and sister. My mother sits in the inner ring on a bench to the left and not far from Brenna, our chief relaxed but powerful on her chair directly in front of the fire.

As the clapping slowly fades, Brenna speaks loudly addressing the entire house. 'Clan of Warham, people of the Iceni. Today a child of ours returns home. We welcome her back with open arms, now ready to make her way as an adult in our family.' She smiles at me and nods her head. I smile and bow in return. 'Cara and Solinus will certainly be hungry from their long journey, so let us feast!'

And with that pronouncement, many people bustle around from the back row and move to the great iron cooking pots, carrying bowls and spoons. My father ushers me over to a bench on the edge of the inside ring. It feels so strange sitting here; I wonder if I will ever get used to this. Will I? Do I want to?

The cooks ladle great scoops into the bowls and serve first Solinus, then me. Then Brenna, my father and mother, and then move on to serve the inside ring. It's so important in our clan to follow the customs. Our council meets often, adjusting rules and customs where it makes sense, but many of these – such as gathering rituals – don't really change much over time.

I dig into my bowl of stew, realising at last that I am ravenously hungry, my stomach growling in relief at a proper meal after so many days of travelling. Bread and cheese are handed out – again in the same order as the stew – and I devour them gratefully. I am more than halfway done when I finally look up from my food and notice the many soft conversations happening around the room. There is warm laughter from time to time and a general sense of well-being.

Drustan leans over my shoulder and startles me by asking, 'How is it?'

'How is what?' I ask him.

'The food of course, silly,' he says. 'Is it similar to what you've been eating?'

I had been so hungry I forgot to stop and taste, but now I realise that the food reminds me most of home. The smells, the tastes – those memories of the senses are so much stronger than anything else we experience.

'Mm, it is delicious,' I say finally. 'It tastes of home.'

He smiles, happy with that answer.

I see that Brenna is moving around now, in anticipation of what will come next. The bards move to the front of the fire ready to entertain us with stories and song. This was always my favourite part of celebrations as a child. Only a bard can tell a story with such feeling and emotion that you feel you are actually in it. I settle in to enjoy the tale, but first my father stands in front and reminds me why we are there.

'Carassouna, if you will join me please,' he says.

I stand, feeling awkward and full, and walk over to the fire. The sky has been darkening outside, and now the light from the fire makes my ornaments glow radiantly in the dim light.

'As you have successfully completed your fosterage, you are now a full member of the clan of Warham. We wish to welcome you with a gift, which we hope you will use wisely and well.' He motions to a boy standing over to the side holding a bundle of blankets, and the boy carries them over. My father unwraps them carefully.

Inside lies the most beautiful sword I have ever seen. The steel face gleams, the polished blade reflecting the light from the fire. The hilt is made from wood and bronze, with an intricately carved handle of swirls and knots. My father puts both hands underneath the sword and lifts it, holds it up to the gathering, then turns and presents it to me.

Holding my breath, I stretch out my hands and he lays the sword on them. I can feel its weight and heft as my arms tighten to balance it. I bow to him over the sword.

'Thank you,' I say. 'I am honoured.' Then I turn to the crowd and address them. 'And thank you to all of you. I hope I will make you proud.' This is met with huge applause and much cheering, as my father tightens a belt around my waist and I awkwardly put the sword into the scabbard.

'I'll show you how to look after it later,' my father says to me quietly with a small smile. The weight instantly feels as though it's pulling me to the ground – thank goodness I don't have to wear this all the time! I return to my seat as gracefully as I can, flushed and awkward, as the bards move front and centre.

I can barely focus as the first story floats through the air in a dream before me. Although everyone gets a sword when they return from fosterage, I've never seen anyone given quite so grand a sword. Have these ceremonies changed while I've been gone? Or is this a sign of things to come, what is meant for me?

I try to push the thoughts aside and turn my mind to the story. Then the bards bring out their instruments. Singing – this will clear my mind. And I happily join in, with melodies as familiar as breathing.

THREE

The next morning, I wake to a still, heavy air.

Birdsong outside tells me it's only daybreak, but already the heat is upon us – it's going to be a sweltering day.

I can hear my mother up and moving around on the other side of the curtain that partitions off my sleeping area. I lie in bed, listening to the sounds of Mam heating water and kneading bread, the slow and steady breathing of my brother and sister still asleep in the sleeping quarter next to me, and the far-off sounds of horses and livestock rising from their slumber, ready to begin a new day.

Here I am, back in my own home, in my bed, after all these seasons. Only it isn't my own bed – Lucilia is now in my old bed, with Mato in hers. This new bed and sleeping area have been added specially for my arrival back home. I can see they've put in a great deal of effort to make it nice for me: a beautifully woven blanket in dark blue, green and yellow plaid must have been a huge effort for my mam, and it perfectly complements the thick sky-blue curtains with golden thread running through. It's amazing what colours she can achieve with her dyeing techniques.

That's something I have in common with Mam at least – we both find it fascinating the different dyes, tinctures and treatments we can make with herbs, roots, flowers and lichen. She has a real gift for finding new ways to use things and discovering new possibilities. I hope to learn from her and improve my skills with plants.

As I roll over and pull my blanket back over my shoulders, I bury my head underneath and think back to the night before. The gathering held in one's honour happens only at very special times: once when returning from fosterage; when and if you're married; and then, if you're lucky, once you reach the elder years of wisdom. I've seen quite a few gatherings as a child, and of course others with the Trinovantes, but I can't recall having seen quite such a magnificent sword before.

I peek out from under my blanket to spy the sword lying carefully perched against my shelves. It's resplendent in its beautifully crafted scabbard. I can only guess this means my father and Brenna are serious about me becoming the next chief...

'Cara,' my mother calls softly from the other side of the curtain. 'Are you awake?'

I wonder if I should stay silent, to keep hold of my

daydreaming time for just a little longer…but if it's this hot already, I think I'd better get started on my work as soon as possible.

'Good morning, Mam,' I call as cheerily as I can. 'Just trying to remember where I put everything.' And that is the truth. At least I've laid some things on the shelves already. I finally throw back the covers and quickly get organised and dressed.

As I walk through the blue curtains into the main area of the roundhouse, I can smell the bread baking. Mam has made me warm honey milk – she hasn't forgotten my favourite special drink.

'Thank you, Mam,' I say as I gratefully take the steamy mug of sweetness from her.

'Have you slept well?' she asks as she walks around behind me and starts to comb my hair.

'It's okay, Mam,' I say and gently push away the comb. 'I've been doing that on my own for a while now.'

'Oh, of course,' she says awkwardly and puts the comb down, 'you're welcome to use my mirror…' She smiles. 'My sweet darling, it's going to be hard for me to get used to you being so grown up now.'

I smile back at her, knowing she means well but feeling a bit irritated nonetheless.

'Don't worry,' I reassure her. 'I don't mind.'

She sits down on one of the benches near the fire and I join her there, taking a sip of my drink. It's just as

I remember.

'Delicious as always, thank you,' I tell her truthfully. 'I did sleep well. Thank you for my new bed, Mam – it's lovely.'

'Oh, I'm so happy you like it,' she says, looking pleased. 'You know I've always loved blue for you – it sets off your hair so beautifully.' She touches my hair.

I can, in fact, remember her telling me this all the time.

'I do like the blue,' I say, 'and also the green…'

'Yes, well it needed another colour as well,' she interjects, 'but isn't the blue just gorgeous, and the curtains I've made using a new formula…I used older woad leaves, which tend to give a lighter colour, and then added just a bit of elderberry at the end of the soaking time – and a bit of extra hot water as well to really draw out the colour. Can you believe, it made such a beautiful shade of blue!'

'I thought it was different than I'd seen before,' I say to her.

A little voice from behind me speaks up, 'Mam made it specially for you – she tried a hundred different ways before she got it right!'

Mam blushes as I turn around to see Mato standing in front of his curtain, still in his sleeping clothes.

'Yes, Mato, thank you,' she says, still blushing. And to me, 'I think he must have overheard Lucilia – she's been telling everyone this.'

She goes over and scoops him up in her arms. 'And how are you, my little bear?' she asks, with a kiss on the cheek. He giggles and scrunches up his shoulders, lying his head against her chest. 'Little Mato here has been so excited for you to come home so he can finally go out to the woods,' she tells me.

'Hurrah!' cheers Mato, and he claps his hands together.

'What's all the cheering about?' Lucilia asks sleepily, rubbing her eyes as she too emerges from her curtain in her sleeping clothes.

'The woods, the woods!' yells Mato.

'I was just telling your sister how excited Mato is about his first trip to the woods with the children,' my mother says to her.

Lucilia looks at me, searchingly. I can see she's wondering how I'll react. It's usually this way – the older children looking after the younger children. And now, of course, I'm an older child and I will be responsible for them in many ways. Our life isn't easy – starvation is a real thing, as is freezing in the cold or dying from illness. Although that all seems so far away right now, with the heat of summer upon us and the harvest underway. We have to work together as a clan to survive, and the children – young and old – have important roles to play.

The problem is, it all seems so boring to me now. Surely a future chief wouldn't feel this way? Surely I would be putting my clan's needs before my own? But all I can think of is riding off on Morna, destination: adventure.

I quickly put a stop to my daydream. It isn't possible anyway, it's much too dangerous for me to ride off alone. I give Lucilia the biggest smile I can muster. This is my family. This is what matters.

'Yes Mato,' I say, 'we will go to the woods. Let's get ready.'

Half an hour later, the little ones are fed and dressed, and we set off from our roundhouse: each of them with a small wicker basket in their hands for twigs or food we may find, and me with a large wicker basket strapped to my back for wood. As we pass by Brenna's roundhouse on our way to the common area, I try to sneak a peek through the doorway but all I can see is the fire burning and empty benches surrounding it. That would explain why Tad wasn't home – they must have gone out already this morning.

We reach the common area and see Senni and a young girl already waiting there, along with two boys who look even older than me. Mato runs towards the young girl while Senni greets us cheerfully and introduces the girl to me as her little sister, Minervina, just four winters.

'Mato and I are best friends,' she tells me secretively.

'I won't tell,' I whisper back to her with a smile.

The biggest boy shyly asks me how I'm getting on, and I tell him it's fine so far.

'Let me know if you need anything,' he says to me.

'Just your name to start,' I say jokingly.

'Andecarus,' he answers. 'Don't you remember? We used to play together every day. But I left six winters ago, so it has been a long time since you've seen me.'

'I'm sorry,' I tell him embarrassedly. 'I am so sorry. I really am having a hard time remembering everyone.'

The other boy, much more aggressive than the first, says, 'Well we wouldn't expect you to know who we are, the great and powerful Carassouna.' The way he says it reminds me of the one child who was always picking on me – Vastini.

'Well, good to know you haven't changed,' I say to him. 'What was your name…Vondeti?' I say, purposefully getting his name wrong.

He turns red and looks ready to let me know his mind when Drustan rushes up.

'Sorry to keep you,' he says breathlessly. I smile at my old friend, glad he's coming along too even though he doesn't have any younger siblings.

'It's okay,' says Senni, taking charge, 'but let's get going now – it's so hot already.'

We pass through the entrance gates, guarded at all times by sentries in the watchtowers. We wave to the guards as we pass. Although full-on attacks are rare, I know that raids and challenges happen often between clans. I've been lucky enough never to experience one yet – probably because we are so far north here and my fosterage clan was so wealthy and powerful, no one dared to challenge them. Leaving the safety of the hillfort always makes me feel a bit nervous…but mostly excited.

Senni leads us west out of the hillfort. 'We've been taking the river path out to the valley woods,' she tells me. 'There's no flooding at the moment, and the sheep are in low pastures so we can check them while we pass.'

I bring up the rear of the group, happy for some space to think, sometimes carrying Mato when he falls behind the others. He's heavy and solid, but he's a sweet little guy and I'm happy for the chance to get to know him a bit more.

We reach the river Stiffkey and follow alongside as it winds its way around the hillfort and then off to the north, towards the sea. There's a gentle breeze blowing now like a soft whisper, rustling my hair and dress ever so slightly. It feels so refreshing whenever I catch it, a cooling break from the hot sun bearing down.

Drustan lingers towards the back as well, and eventually settles into step beside me. 'You're very quiet today,' he says suddenly, breaking into my thoughts.

'Just enjoying the silence,' I reply.

'Oh,' he says and falls silent.

'Sorry,' I say to him, 'that wasn't a hint.'

He smiles.

'I was just thinking…there's a lot to take in,' I tell him.

I adjust the wicker basket on my back – the straps are

really digging into my shoulders already, and it isn't even full yet.

We walk on, and soon reach the cover of trees for some relief. I kneel by the river to take a drink and help Mato get a drink as well.

'Let's set up here,' Senni says.

We set our baskets in a circle, gauging how much wood we'll need, then quickly split up to get the job done as quickly as possible.

Vastini grumbles as soon as Senni mentions cutting wood. 'I'll just stay here and keep an eye on everyone,' he says.

'Not likely!' Senni says with a snort, and drags both him and Andecarus off towards a fallen tree, brandishing her axe for good effect. Mato and Minervina begin gathering twigs in their little baskets. Lucilia wanders off on her own, searching for some berries, while Drustan heads off to check the fish traps in the river.

I start to gather twigs with the little ones and laugh as they make silly faces with some of the moss they find on the fallen logs. I do a face too, and a silly voice, and Mato seems to think it's the funniest thing ever.

'Cara,' a voice speaks up from behind me. I jump, startled that Lucilia has come up so quietly.

'Lucy, I thought you went off in search of berries,' I say.

'Oh yes, I have a secret trove,' she says, and lifts up the

41

scarf covering her basket to reveal a huge pile of blackberries and some damsons.

'That's amazing!' I exclaim, to which she looks very pleased. She covers the fruit back up to keep it from wasps, then looks serious again.

'I wanted to talk with you,' she says, 'about – you know.' Puzzled, I stare blankly at her. 'You know – going away...' she stutters, looking close to tears.

'Oh Lucy,' I say gently, not sure if I should hug her or keep my distance. It's hard being away from someone for so long – you miss out on the little nuances of their personality, how they respond to touch, how their emotions work.

I decide hugging is better than not, so reach out and pull her to me. She bursts into tears and I hug her tighter. Poor little Mato looks so sad, as though he might cry himself, but I reassure him she'll be fine.

After a long few minutes of heart-wrenching sobs, interspersed with sniffles and gulps of breath, I let go of her a bit and look at her.

'Sweet Lucy,' I say, 'I didn't know you were so worried!'

She nods, her small, heart-shaped face covered in red splotches.

'I know there isn't much I can do or change for you,' I say to her. 'But Mam and Tad know you so well, they wouldn't send you anywhere that wasn't good for you.'

'But you went so far away!' she cries.

'But that's unusual,' I reassure her quickly. 'Most likely you will go very near – in fact, we must talk about this together, they need to know you don't want to go far away.'

'Oh, but I couldn't bring it up,' she says worriedly.

'You must be brave,' I tell her. 'Have courage.' I take her hand. 'I'll be there with you. We'll talk about it tonight.'

She looks at me uncertainly, then gives me a shy little smile and nods. I gently wipe the stray tears from her cheeks and push her hair back a little from her face. She is such a sweet, sincere person. I can see her balancing her composure in a way much advanced for her seasons.

'Fish!' comes a call from upstream.

We all hurry over to see Drustan hooking and hauling out one…two…three fish! 'Pretty well-sized, too,' he says, holding them up proudly.

I clap for him and the little ones join in.

'What's happening over here?' asks Senni as she and the older boys walk over the slight rise that heads towards the heart of the wood.

Drustan holds up the catch and says, 'We're doing well today!'

'You call that a fish?' Vastini says, jeeringly, 'I've seen bigger tadpoles.'

We all roll our eyes.

'You go catch a bigger one yourself then,' Senni says to him. 'Well done,' she says to Drustan, 'I think we have enough wood. Let's have our lunch then we can head back.'

Andecarus comes into his own now – he takes out a huge loaf of bread from his cloak and several hunks of cheese. I suddenly realise my stomach is growling quite loudly.

'I think we're all hungry,' Drustan says with a smile as he wades back onto shore near me.

'Very funny,' I say and punch him on the arm.

Lucilia seems a bit more cheerful next to me now and pulls back the scarf so the others can see the berries and fruit in her basket.

'Ooh,' breathes Senni, 'you really are outdoing yourself, Lucy!'

'Right – let's eat,' says Drustan and we arrange ourselves comfortably in a little circle, sharing out food and passing around the water flask. Vastini grumpily sits down and joins in, forsaking the fishing challenge for now.

Silence falls over the group as we steadily work our way through the picnic. I get up at one point to refill the flask, and realise I am content for the first time since arriving home. The nerves are finally fading away.

Back in the circle, I ask the older boys what their fosterage was like.

'Oh, much the same as everyone else's,' says Andecarus, looking quite nonchalant.

Vastini, on the other hand, doesn't look very happy to

be talking about it, so I quickly change the subject before anything can be said that will make Lucilia more unhappy.

'How about a float?' I ask.

'I'm game,' Drustan says, jumping to his feet.

'It *is* much too hot today,' says Senni a bit reluctantly, wanting to keep us focused on our work. But she concedes, 'Probably best to cool off before heading home, I suppose.'

'Race you!' Drustan calls, pulling off layers as he runs towards the river.

I help Mato and Minervina to their feet, then we run together towards the river, Lucilia and Senni following leisurely behind.

Drustan is already in the water by the time we reach the edge, and we take off layers down to our underclothes and shirts before wading in. The first laps of the water feel cold around my ankles and legs, but as I immerse myself, I quickly adjust to the temperature. It has been a hot summer, but the river moves so quickly it never really gets that warm. Drustan splashes me playfully and I splash him back, then make sure the little ones are okay in the shallows. Senni, Lucilia and the older boys are all coming in now, and we play around, ducking under and springing back up, playing tag and generally splashing as much as we can.

One of us always stays towards shore with the little ones – who especially love to stick their toes in and then run away – but Lucilia can pretty much keep up with the rest of us. I move out to the centre of the river and float lazily on my back, looking up at the sparkling light filtering through the leaves. I feel at peace in this magical place.

Suddenly, something tickles the back of my leg and I startle, thinking it's a fish. But then Drustan circles around to my head and says, 'Only me.'

'You scared me!' I splutter, and splash him as my float is broken. I move onto my back again and he stays near my head, looking at me. 'Yes?' I say, not sure what he's up to.

'I missed you, you know,' he says to me, quietly.

'I missed you too,' I say automatically.

'Oh no, you didn't,' he replies in a strange voice. 'Not really, not the same way.' My heart beats a little faster, and I look at him out of the corner of my eye.

'Which way is that?' I ask.

But he doesn't answer, just treads water, then floats up onto his back and drifts slightly away from me.

'Okay, we really do need to go now!' Senni calls out suddenly. 'We don't want anyone to worry.'

I pop back up in the water. She is standing near shore, her turn with the little ones, watching Drustan and I warily. I wonder if she could hear our conversation.

I know she's right, but it's so hard dragging myself out of the water. It seems the second I fully emerge, the water evaporates as the heat of the day kicks in.

We dress quickly, now feeling the urgency to get back home. We gather our baskets and start off again, following the river and staying under the cover of trees for as long as possible. When we finally have to break cover, we can feel the sun beating upon our necks. The little ones have to stop often for a drink of water.

With everyone feeling hot and uncomfortable, the conversation quickly becomes more confrontational. Soon Vastini, Andecarus, Senni and Drustan are arguing over whose sword-fighting skills are the best.

'After training with the Trinovantes, I reckon I'd probably win that contest,' I join in.

'You!' snorts Vastini. 'But you're only just twelve! No way you could beat me.'

'I don't know about that,' laughs Drustan, 'you're pretty scrawny.'

Vastini grabs Drustan and tries to wrestle him down to the ground.

'Well, let's just see about that, shall we?' I say loudly, ignoring a little voice in my head telling me to stop. What am I getting myself into? 'Maybe not sword fighting, but archery should be easy enough to test.'

They both stop and look at me, then see I'm serious and straighten up.

'What do you propose?' asks Vastini, sauntering over to me.

'A hunting expedition,' I retort. 'On the day of the

next new moon. The first one with a wild boar is the winner – and has the honour of presenting a feast to the clan.'

'Deal,' says Vastini. 'We'll all take part.'

'Any excuse for an outing,' says Andecarus, rolling his eyes at his friend.

I try to smile boldly, but inside feel shaky and uncertain. Why did I do that? I want to prove myself worthy of the expectations on me – but what if I don't succeed? All of the relaxed feeling I managed to get that day drains from my body. I must succeed.

FOUR

The day of the new moon dawns grey and overcast, a mist rising from the valley below. Even before I wake, it feels my mind is preparing me for the day ahead. For this is the day of the hunt.

I've been trying to squeeze in extra riding time for the past month, Morna and I heading out at any opportunity to work on our jumps, our stops, our turns – our connection. She is a true companion, the best horse I've ever ridden, and I know I'm in safe hands with her. Senni, Drustan and I have been working more diligently in our normal training as well: with target practice for accuracy, running and sparring for stamina and spear throwing for strength.

We're lucky to be in the hillfort – we don't have to spend much time in the fields. With the long days of summer and all the crops ripening, this is the peak harvest period. Anyone in the farmsteads who is able to work is called into service to help with the harvest. But ours is the life of the warrior, the life we've been born into. We train alongside our daily jobs: gathering wood; foraging for berries, mushrooms and wild herbs; caring for livestock; weaving; cooking; looking after the younger children – this is what we do when we've returned from fosterage, before we are full-fledged warriors.

This hunting expedition today wouldn't be unusual, were it not for the challenge attached to it. Although I suppose that's not unusual either – I'm certainly not the first person ever to speak before thinking! But I can't seem to stop my anxiety; knowing it is my challenge, especially, makes this all the more meaningful.

On the positive side, it has turned into an excuse to spend lots of time with my friends. I've so enjoyed the time we've spent getting to know each other again; I feel lucky to have them on my side.

As I get dressed for the day, I can hear low voices outside my sleeping area. Mam and Senni poke their heads through.

'Senovara's here to help you get ready, Carassouna,' my mam announces, and smiles at her. 'What a good friend.'

Senni looks happy with this pronouncement and bustles over to my side, eyeing me up and down and turning me round so she can see me from all sides. 'Hmm…' she says, 'not quite the right colours…'

What is it with these people and colours? Why do they always want me to wear…

'Blue, that's what you need to wear,' she pronounces confidently. 'It sets off your hair and eyes so perfectly.'

I roll my eyes when she can't see, but decide to give in – she is my friend after all and only has my best interests at heart.

Senni chooses a whole new outfit for me, complete with full ornamentation – torc, bracelets and armband. As she works, I sit on the bed and watch her fondly. I wonder, 'You haven't told me much about your time away yet, Senni. We've had so much time together in training lately, but you haven't spoken about it much.'

She's quiet for a moment, and I wonder if she's heard me, but then she puts down the new tunic she's chosen and looks straight into my eyes. 'You're right,' she says finally. 'We haven't discussed it – I wondered if you were interested at all.'

'I'm sorry…' I start to say, but she cuts me off and brusquely says, 'You don't need to apologise, we've all been busy.'

Her words sting and I recoil, stunned. I've never heard her speak this way and wonder where my friend has gone.

I must look shocked, because she sighs deeply and sits down heavily on the bed next to me. After a moment of silence, she softly says, 'I know deep down you care, but it's hard always being in your shadow.'

My heart sinks and I feel a pit deep down in my stomach. In my shadow? How could she feel this way? I never knew…

'Oh Senni, why didn't you tell me?' I cry out to her, tears welling up in my eyes. 'I feel so awful – I never meant you to feel that way.' One tear breaks free and slides down my cheek; I taste its saltiness as it reaches the corner of my mouth.

'How long have you felt this way?' I ask quietly.

She looks at me carefully and answers seriously, 'As long as I can remember.'

I let out a little cry, and she hurries on, 'Cara, I know you never meant for this to happen. It's just the way things are; just the way our lives have happened.'

She takes my hand and gives me a little smile then continues, 'Anyway, I was with the clan of Thornham – do you know them? Very near the sea, up past the forest at Brancaster. They eat fish much more than land animals; different fish to what we find in the river here. It was another world, living so close to the huge waters. I liked to sit on the shore, gazing out at the vast expanse and watching the waves roll in – sometimes so gently they seemed to whisper; other times foaming giants crashing into the land.'

She sighs, and I can see in her eyes that she has travelled back there in her mind. 'And so much time actually out at sea, on their little boats. I loved it – loved the peacefulness of that vast space, and the changeable nature of the sea. Whenever I needed to think, I would go and sit near the sea, just watching the waves roll in and feeling the flow of the earth.'

She stops remembering then and looks at me. 'It really made me feel like I finally understood myself, like I was finally happy just being me.'

Her eyes are welling up now too, and a few silent tears escape and roll down her cheeks. We cry together, and I am still for a moment as I take in what she's telling me. Then I do the only thing I can think of – reach over and embrace my friend in the warmest hug I can give.

'My dear friend,' I say, 'you must know how loved you are. No one could ever replace you. Besides,' I add, 'no one else can get us out of trouble quite the way you can.'

We both laugh and pull apart, wiping our eyes. 'Speaking of getting out of trouble,' I say, 'how am I going to get out of this mess I'm in today?'

'Cara,' she says, 'you can do this, I know you can. I've seen you ride. I've seen you shoot. I'll be there by your side.'

'Thank you,' I say and squeeze her hand warmly, appreciating her friendship.

'We should go now though,' she says. 'It's almost time to meet; hurry and get ready.'

I quickly change into the clothes and ornaments Senni has laid out for me, then she leads me out into the main area of the roundhouse.

As I walk through the curtains, my mam lets out a gasp. 'Oh Senni, you have dressed her well!' she exclaims.

Mam picks up the mirror from her dressing table and brings it over to me, that I might see Senni's work. As I look in the mirror, I see myself in surprise. Where did my child self go? The face reflected there looks older, wiser – and much stronger than I realised. But the blue eyes looking back at me are still the same, and there I see myself.

'You are full of grace,' my mother says, coming up behind me and smoothing my hair back, the beads threaded throughout gently tapping together. I turn and give her a tight hug, grateful for a moment of safety in her arms.

When I pull away, I feel my determination renewed. 'Right,' I say. 'It's time; we must go.'

I gather my bow, arrows and quiver, then Senni and I leave the warmth and safety of my family roundhouse for the uncertainty of the forest.

We set off first for the stables and find that Andecarus and Vastini have beaten us there, with their horses almost ready to ride.

'Nice of you to join us, Cara,' Vastini says sarcastically and I give him a look.

'We aren't in any hurry,' I reply, 'the boar will be waiting for us.'

If only I felt so sure…at least I can put on my confidence; I mustn't let him know how nervous I feel inside.

A voice calls out, 'Is that Cara and Senni here?' Drustan walks around from behind a feed store, then stops in his tracks, speechless.

'Drustan, are you okay?' I ask, worriedly rushing over to him. He turns bright red and his mouth closes, looking down.

'Um, yes, sorry,' he says. He looks up at me and I can see his cheeks visibly flush again. He clears his throat. 'I haven't seen you wear that tunic before,' he says. Vastini and Andecarus laugh, and I feel embarrassed myself.

'Oh, it's just something Senni picked out for me,' I say, secretly pleased now that I listened to her advice. I am starting to wonder how Drustan really feels about me – and how I feel about him.

'Morna,' Senni says, breaking into my thoughts and through the slightly awkward silence that has sprung up between Drustan and I.

'Yes, right,' I say, and hurry over to where Morna waits, stroking my clever horse as she playfully nuzzles my arm and cheek, making me laugh.

I get Morna ready to ride as Senni tends to her horse, then we lead them out of the stables, through the common area and towards the entrance of the hillfort. Many people call out best wishes for speed, luck and safety. I am bolstered somewhat by their kindness, but still feel my stomach twisted into knots with nerves. What if I can't find a boar? What if Vastini beats me to it? What if I don't shoot as well as he does? What will my friends and family think if I lose this challenge?

I see Brenna standing at the door to her roundhouse as we pass; she simply waves and calls out 'Good speed to you,' then disappears back inside.

Mam and the little ones have come to the hillfort entrance to see us off, and my siblings hug me and pat Morna as we walk past, while Mam gives me a quick kiss on the forehead. 'Be safe, my dearest,' she says.

Outside the entrance, we meet up with the others and mount our horses, then set off to the starting point on the edge of the forest, one league away. We keep to a walk to conserve the horses' energy for the hunt. The mist is a thick fog out here, especially on the hills. As we come into a valley, we get a momentary clearing to see some of our surroundings before plunging back into fog again. No one speaks as we travel, our thoughts our own.

It's dangerous to travel in these conditions, not able to see what could spring on us from beyond. There are also dangers in this task. Boar are unpredictable, and very strong. Rival clans may be passing through the forest. We may not be prepared for all we could face.

After a tense journey, we approach the forest and stop near a thicket of giant, gnarled oak trees, only the faint traces of a path visible on the ground. We all know these woods well, the thick clumps of trees cut through only here and there by narrow paths; the mossy, damp smell; the silence broken occasionally by a shuffle of leaves or the song of a bird. But today the mist has settled deeply, and we can only see in by about the length of a person.

We, too, are silent until Drustan says, 'Perhaps this should wait until tomorrow – I'm not sure how successful anyone will be in this fog. I thought it would have cleared by now.'

'Hhmpf,' snorts Vastini, 'it's not so bad.' But his face tells another story. I must not be the one to back down.

'No,' I say, 'we will go. You don't need to – the rest of you should stay here while Vastini and I go; after all, we don't want to trample over each other,' I say with a half-hearted laugh, trying to make light of the situation.

'We won't leave you,' Senni says, moving her horse to stand next to mine.

'Of course not,' Drustan agrees emphatically.

I feel grateful to my friends and try to give them a smile – but I can feel how weak it is, betraying my nervousness. My brain is racing, as is my heart, but I know I must focus if I am to succeed.

I force myself to take a few deep breaths while I lean down and whisper to Morna, stroking her neck while she nibbles at some branches. She lets out a whinny, tossing her head and looking back towards me, and I think this is her encouragement. She knows me so well.

'Right, let's get started,' I say and lead the group into the mist.

Inside the forest, the fog is patchier, clearing in some of the lowland areas. Morna and I try to follow the faint paths, making as little noise as possible in the brush and fallen leaves. She steps surely over the obstacles in our path – a fallen tree, a bramble bush – but I worry for the time when we will have to run. I can see the others scattered throughout the wood nearby, moving in and out of mist like phantoms, seemingly gliding through the trees. We stop every so often to examine broken branches and tree marks, looking for signs or tracks of the boar.

I start to feel slightly disoriented – although I know this forest so well, our closest one, the mist is making me lose all sense of direction. I see a marked tree I'm pretty sure is the same one I made note of when we first came in.

Suddenly, I hear a whinnying and snorts from off to my left, about thirty cubits away, then a scamper and the sound of leaves and bushes being trampled in a frantic scramble. A call comes out – the call of the hunt – and I know that Vastini has found one.

'Come,' I call out to Morna, quickly tapping her sides with my heels. We turn in the direction of the scrambling noise and set off at a run. The trees fly past as Morna gives chase, and I ride low. I can feel the damp air clinging to me as we ride quickly through the patches of fog, and I hold my breath through each one, hoping a hidden danger doesn't present itself.

Out again now, and I can see the figures of Drustan off to my left and Andecarus even further behind and out. I hear a whooping call behind me to my right and know that is Senni, also giving chase. Vastini must still be up ahead.

We are fast approaching the riverbed, and I speak to Morna encouragingly about the coming jump. I know there is a perfect crossing point from this part of the forest, if only we can find the right place.

Back in to the fog, and I have to steer us towards the river based on memory. I can hear now the sounds of Vastini up ahead, and at the next break I see him – even closer than I realised. I feel a boost of confidence as I realise that Morna and I are definitely the better riding team; in clear conditions, we would've been ahead long before now.

He glances behind him and sees me just over his shoulder, urging his horse on. But it's not enough – Morna and I take the lead and I steer her deftly towards the spot I think we need to jump. One hundred cubits…fifty…we move into the fog again at just the wrong time and I panic not knowing if I'm at the right spot.

The fog clears just before we reach the river and I suddenly realise I'm one river bend further along than I thought. It's too late now, we'll have to jump or risk going in the river. I think we can make it...

I brace myself against Morna and she takes off from the bank, stretching wide towards the other side. Her front legs easily clear the ledge on the other bank, then I glance back to see her back legs come down just slightly low on the bank. I hold on tightly as she scrambles up the mud and brush to gain a solid hold on the top.

Phew. That was close. Mustn't stop now – grunts just up ahead catch my attention. The boar would have scrambled down the bank and quickly splashed through the river, but I'm surprised it was able to climb the steep bank so quickly.

I take off in pursuit, the fog clearing again, and I get my first glimpse of the catch. A beautiful boar, quite small still but with tusks, probably just a teen himself. I reach for my bow.

Behind me I hear a shout and a cry, then scared and fearful whinnying, and I turn to see Vastini and his horse disappear over the edge of the bank. My heart leaps into my mouth – he hasn't made the jump. The boar is just up ahead. But I can't leave Vastini.

Morna and I turn quickly and move back to the edge of the river bed. I dismount just before and carefully walk up to the edge, calling to him that I'm coming. I look down and see that his horse is back on her feet, uninjured, but Vastini is lying at the bottom of the slope, unmoving.

I can't see his face and call to him again, then scramble down as quickly as I can without falling. When I reach him, I can see he is breathing, his eyes closed.

'Vastini,' I say again and his eyelids flicker open. He seems to recognise me, and I sit back with relief. 'What happened there?' I ask, putting on an upbeat voice. He groans as he tries to sit up, and I gently ease him back again. 'I don't think you should sit up just yet, that was quite a fall you had.'

'She just couldn't make it,' he croaks, his voice hoarse and parched. I hand him my water flask for a drink. He speaks again, this time sounding more like himself. 'Her front legs landed, but the back just couldn't get a grip on this mud. She slid down and I was thrown off.'

Now the others have arrived on the opposite bank, and Drustan and Senni hurry down while Andecarus holds the horses. I realise I've left Morna on her own, but glance up to see her watching over us.

'What are you doing here, anyway?' Vastini asks, suddenly gruff. 'Shouldn't you have caught the boar by now?' I can sense the hurt pride in his voice.

'I had it in sight and was about to draw…but then I heard you,' I reply.

'You had it in sight and didn't take a shot,' he repeats incredulously, looking at me in a new light. His cheeks flush red. 'I…I didn't realise you would do that for me,' he says. I don't respond, wondering if he would have done the same for me but knowing it doesn't really matter – there's no way I could leave someone injured, even if it is my fiercest competitor.

'You're certainly talking well enough now,' I say. 'Let's see if you can stand.'

Drustan has been deftly checking Vastini over while we were talking and nods to me. 'I can't feel anything broken,' he says.

'No blood either as far as I can see,' I say.

Senni collects the things that have fallen – Vastini's bow, arrows, quiver, cloak – and gathers the horse's reins. Drustan and I brace Vastini under both arms and help pull him to his feet.

'How does that feel?' I ask.

'Very sore,' he replies. 'Everything hurts; but I'll live. Now how about that boar? Any idea which way it went?'

I shake my head and laugh, relieved this wasn't more serious.

'A better question,' says Senni, 'is how are we going to get out of here?' She gestures to the steep banks on either side.

I look up and down the river and can't see a way for Vastini's horse to climb up, but then Andecarus calls out from downriver, 'Here! There's a spot here.'

I turn to Vastini. 'Can you walk?' I ask. 'I have to get Morna.'

'I think so,' he says, and gives it a try, leaning heavily

on Drustan. 'Yes, I think I can walk.'

I climb up the steep bank and Senni hands up Vastini's things, then I lead Morna over to the spot Andecarus has found. He's right, here the land dips to provide gentle inlets to climb in and out. He's already led the other horses down and is waiting for everyone.

Vastini is able to move with surprising speed – he's tougher than I realised – and they catch up with us before too long, then climb up the side to where I stand waiting. Drustan and Vastini come up last, Drustan helping to push him from behind while I help pull him up the slope. He seems to be recovering, and with it his arrogance returns.

He takes the reins from Senni and asks her for a foot up in the saddle, wincing with the effort.

'Good, well…' Vastini looks around impatiently. 'What are we waiting for?' That statement sends us into action, stunned a bit by the tone. Seems Vastini is going to be fine after all.

Somewhat annoyed by his lack of gratitude, I mount Morna, wait for the others to mount and set off with renewed determination. I'm going to be more diligent in my tracking this time.

I was the last one to see the boar, so I sense the others waiting for me to make a move. 'Well, she was definitely in that clearing through there,' I say, pointing ahead. We all move in that direction and start tracking.

The fog has cleared somewhat in this section of forest, and I can already see some marks on trees to the right of the clearing. I start off swiftly in that direction, urging Morna to move as quickly and nonchalantly as possible. I don't want to give away what I've seen too early.

We quickly trot away from the group down the slope from the clearing, then crest the mound on the other side. Out of the corner of my eye, a motion – dark, round, rumbling low to the earth. My heart quickens. I glance quickly behind me but don't see anyone following me yet. I lean down and whisper to Morna, 'We must be very quiet girl. Step gingerly.'

I ease her forward, staying on the soil and away from the fallen leaves littering the ground as much as possible. We get to a spot very near a giant ash tree, majestic in its multiple trunks and eight-foot base. I peer around carefully and see that the boar is there on the other side, poking around in the leaves about twenty cubits away in a little ring of trees, obviously feeling it has made it to safety.

I draw my bow from the quiver and reach in for an arrow. This is the true test. The life of an animal for the life of people. My people will use every bit of this animal – a feast for the clan; the skin dried and cured into shoes and tarps; teeth, claws and bones for weapons and tools. But what of the boar? A beautiful creature being sacrificed. I stretch my arm out, loaded bow in hand, sighting down my arm, down my knuckle, as I draw back the arrow. I can do this. I take a deep breath.

I urge Morna forward, to step out from behind the tree, knowing I will need to take a quick shot before the boar panics. But before I can move out all the way, an arrow flies past me and hits the boar. It has struck, just above the boar's front leg – a perfect shot.

The frightened boar rears up, snorting fiercely, running around in circles. I need to end this quickly so the boar won't suffer – or charge. I take aim but before I can let go, the boar stops. It turns its head and I feel it looking straight at me, through me. I wonder if I should take the shot, but red appears at the sides of its mouth and the boar drops suddenly down to his side.

I look behind me and there is Vastini, riding up towards me. We approach the boar, and can see it has breathed its last; it is done.

We both dismount and together examine the boar, find a sturdy branch to hang it from and prepare to carry it home. The others join us as they arrive, and I'm grateful for the reassuring presence of Senni and Drustan.

Why did I stop? Why did I hesitate? Now I've lost the challenge, and Vastini will return triumphant. Perhaps I'm just not cut out for the warrior way of life.

We ride back home even more slowly than we came, a gentle rain steadily drenching us while we take turns carrying the boar between two of us. I admit my doubts to Senni and Drustan, but they urge me not to doubt myself. They never leave my side.

When we enter the gates, one of the guards calls out and people run from all the nearby houses to come see us and learn the score. Vastini presents the boar to our clan, and at first surprised looks and murmurs pass between many of the watching crowd.

I dismount Morna and walk over to him. 'I offer many congratulations to Vastini,' I begin, 'who has most definitely won the challenge and today brings home the prize.' I shake his hand, and he looks at me meaningfully, seemingly with a new level of respect. He bows to me in return.

Then a great cheer erupts from the crowd as Vastini and Andecarus hoist the boar up between them and carry it, surrounded by cheering clan members, to the main cooking house. There will certainly be a feast tonight.

That evening, I dress for dinner and help Mam prepare the honey beer and herbed bread we're bringing to the celebration. The warm smells of home make me feel safe, secure and loved. I remember, not so long ago, baking herbed bread with my foster mother as we prepared for my farewell feast. I miss her, and my foster father. They were so kind to me, gentle and welcoming. I wonder when I'll see them again?

Mato and Lucilia's arguing breaks me from my reverie, and I give a quick hug to Mam. She looks surprised but pleased, then goes to tend to the little ones.

Once we're all ready, we join the other families gathered in the main meeting house, where food and drink are shared around and stories are told. This time, I've been moved to the back, while Vastini gets a place of honour in the front. My pride is hurt, but it does mean I get to join my friends.

After dinner and stories, the music and singing begins.

As there's still light in the long summer evening, the dancing moves outside. Drustan asks me to dance and I blush, wondering again about his feelings for me – and mine for him.

We weave in and out of the other partners, floating around the space as if we've danced together our whole lives. The stars begin to come out as the sky darkens, the only light left on the horizon, and I think perhaps today isn't so bad after all. I lose myself in the music and the dancing, forgetting all the pressures I've been feeling, all the weight bearing down on me. Tonight, there is only life and magic.

When we finally collapse on the ground laughing, close to the bonfire, I realise that Senni has been watching us.

'That was a beautiful dance,' she admires, her voice sounding a bit funny.

I give her a huge hug which makes her smile a bit. 'I'm

going to get something to drink,' I decide. 'Do you two want anything?'

As I fill up three cups of honey brew, Brenna suddenly appears at my side. 'I've heard about your hunt today… and what you did,' she adds purposefully. I look up, straight into her eyes, and can see there is hope, love and pride. Perhaps all is not lost. 'Come visit me tomorrow,' she says. 'We will talk more then.'

She gives me a smile, then disappears through the dancing crowd. A personal invitation from Brenna. That doesn't happen every day.

FIVE

Every time my mam weaves, I can't help feeling impressed and amazed by what she can do with some clumps of wool and herbs. The process of creating different colours of yarn is one learnt over hundreds of hours of trial and error – and an art she has perfected to a science. She makes beautiful shades of pink, yellow, blue, green, red, orange – a whole rainbow – simply by boiling the right amount of the right plant in water with the wool. Even more than this, she knows how to combine colours and how to make beautiful patterns. I've always had a carefully crafted wardrobe, and I have Mam to thank for that.

Today is a weaving day, so Mam settles down to work at the loom with yarn she's already prepared, while Lucilia busies herself making bread and Mato plays happily outside in the common area with the other small children.

Mam will soon have other women join her for a dyeing session – she is considered the clan expert, so others are keen to learn from her and broaden their knowledge.

Tad is also at home this morning, preparing the stew that Lucilia will tend throughout the day. As an elder of the clan, he's one of the first to be offered meat when it's available; we've been lucky enough to receive a small piece of the boar leftover from the feast. He'll make it go much further by cooking it in water with beans, garlic and barley, seasoned with herbs.

I enjoy the busy, happy sounds of my family working and playing while I get ready for my meeting with Brenna. Although I've known her my entire life, I've not spent much time alone in her company, and I'm worried I'll say or do the wrong thing. I don't know exactly what she wants to talk about – only that it must be important if I've been invited to her house on my own.

When I'm finally ready, I join my family in the main area of the roundhouse. The feeling of home surrounds me – the fire cracking in the hearth, right in the centre of the house, burning constantly. The smoke rising steadily and covering the roof in a layer of soot, helping to keep us warm and dry. The delicious smells of food baking and cooking. The sounds of Mam singing as she weaves, of Tad talking to himself and to Lucilia as he prepares the food, and Lucilia humming along with Mam's singing.

Mato runs in and wraps himself around Tad's leg,

eager for a hug from this great man.

Tad laughs and scoops him up. 'Ah, Mato, young lad, you'll have to be helping around here before too long.'

'Don't rush these things,' my mam interjects, 'we don't want him growing up too quickly and going away from us.'

Lucilia looks suddenly crestfallen. I go over and put my arm around her.

'It's freedom,' I say quietly. 'You will enjoy it.'

'That's right,' Tad booms. 'We all go through it. And we all come back better for it.'

I'm not so sure about that, but I do know I'm different. As much as I love the safe and secure feeling of being home, I long to explore and break free of the hillfort.

I remember my promise from earlier. 'Lucilia has been wanting to talk about her fosterage, actually,' I say loudly, and she turns away suddenly, her face going bright red. 'It's okay,' I whisper reassuringly.

'Lucilia is worried she might be sent far away, as I was,' I begin. 'I told her how unusual that is; I'm sure hers will follow the normal pattern and be nearby, but I thought she would feel better hearing that from you.'

I look from Mam to Tad as they look at each other, and Mam nods almost imperceptibly.

'Of course,' Tad says. 'That's normal to worry.'

He ruffles Lucilia's hair with a smile. 'Nothing to worry about though, my sweet, your mam has that in hand – and she's looking very nearby indeed.'

My mam smiles now and reaches out her hands towards Lucilia, who walks over and takes them. 'It turns out, actually,' Mam says, 'that Gleva could use some help on her farmstead. As you know her so well, I thought perhaps you might enjoy that?'

As Mam finishes, Lucilia bursts into tears and Mam looks shocked. 'Oh no! I thought you would be pleased,' she says. But Lucilia flings her small arms around Mam's neck and squeezes her so that Mam laughs and sputters, 'There, there…' trying gently to loosen her arms.

Lucilia pulls back, her face bright red and streaked with tears, but with a giant smile. 'That's the best idea I've ever heard!' she cries enthusiastically, and we all laugh with relief.

Gleva is Mam's best friend from childhood. They grew up together in farming families, even before the hillfort was built. But Gleva stayed behind near the farm when Mam moved into the hillfort. We've known her all our lives, and she's like a second mother to us. I couldn't have thought of a better place for Lucilia to go.

Mam and Lucilia talk animatedly, but I realise it's time for me to leave for Brenna's.

'I'm off now,' I say loudly to no one in particular, or maybe everyone.

Tad's face suddenly turns from laughing and playful to serious. 'This is very important,' he says to me. 'Don't

72

forget what you have learnt.' Then more lightheartedly, 'Tell my oldest friend to take good care of my oldest daughter. And ask her about the berries,' he adds with a wink.

As Brenna's closest advisor and lead warrior, my father Bellator has the honour of having the second largest roundhouse in the hillfort, very near to Brenna's. As his family, we've grown up with this distinction, although I've hardly ever set foot in her house. To me, it's a mysterious place full of secrets, where urgent meetings are held in hushed tones and heady scents of musk and lavender often fill the air.

With the sun coming around to mid-morning, I approach the large double doors, propped open on this warm summer's day, and enter the house then move directly to the left as is the custom. With the doorway the only source of light into a roundhouse, the people inside can't see the face of anyone standing in the doorway. It's polite to move aside directly and announce yourself, otherwise you're considered rude or even dangerous.

'It is Carassouna Vendi,' I say, 'here to meet with Brenna.'

'Ah, Carassouna,' a voice replies from the darkness somewhere near the middle of the house, a figure coming into focus as my eyes adjust to the dim light inside. It's Brenna, and she is alone.

'Welcome,' she says, moving towards me, arms

outstretched. She places her hands on my arms, just below my shoulders, and looks at me intently, studying me. She smiles warmly. 'So often we are too busy to notice the smaller things, but I can see now how much you resemble your father, my dear friend Bellator. You have his kind eyes.'

She takes my hands in hers and studies them, 'And you have your mother's skilled hands. How wonderful! She is among the finest craftspeople I have ever known.'

'Ever?' I ask in surprise.

Brenna laughs, 'You doubt her skill?'

'No,' I hurriedly reply, 'not at all…I just wouldn't have thought Mam among the best *ever*…'

'Indeed,' Brenna says, 'it's easiest to overlook those we know the best. Come now, let us sit by the fire.'

She leads me further into the roundhouse, and I take in the luxurious surroundings. Thick, red curtains woven with gold flecks separate the main area from the sleeping areas at the back. The large fire pit takes centre stage with two giant iron fire guards, the ends shaped into horses. Placed around the fire are intricately carved wooden benches, the swirls and designs of skilled woodcarving jumping off the surfaces.

We take a seat on the benches, and Brenna sets out a tray with two mugs and plates, then pours an herbal infusion into the mugs and offers one to me. I breathe in the invigorating scent and let the warm steam calm my nerves, then take a careful sip – the delicious taste of mint warms me.

'How is your family today?' Brenna asks me.

'Very well, thank you,' I reply.

'Your father is a very important figure in the life of Warham,' Brenna says, 'as I'm sure you've recognised.'

'Yes,' I agree.

'What does he have to say about our meeting today?' she asks.

I think back to what my father told me before I left.

'He says to remember what I have learnt,' I say. Brenna nods in response. 'And to ask you about the berries?'

She throws back her head in laughter. I hadn't really thought any of this was very important, but obviously it was the right thing to say.

'He knows me very well, your father,' Brenna says. 'You know, we have known each other since we were just tiny babes.'

'Oh yes,' I nod, 'Tad's mentioned that many times.'

'Has he told you much else?' she asks.

'Not really,' I say, 'just a few little pieces here and there…mostly how you have dark hair because your ancestors are from the land of the Ordovices.'

'That's true,' she replies, 'and not just any ancestors – my parents are directly from there. Let me get you something to eat, and I will tell you the story.'

She moves to the far side of the fire, carrying the

tray, and returns with hot, steaming bread on each plate. 'These are the berries your father was referring to – some of the young warriors came across a new patch of berries yesterday, which the elders have inspected for safety. One of them knows this berry from her youth – a strawberry she called it – but has not seen it since that time. We've tested it, just to make sure it's safe to eat, and indeed it is safe…and absolutely delicious! Enjoy.'

'I am honoured,' I say, 'thank you.' The just-baked bread smells delicious and I eagerly take a hungry bite despite the heat. A sweet, juicy burst of fruit hits my mouth, burning the inside slightly but rewarding the pain with its luscious flavour.

'This is unbelievable,' I declare emphatically, and Brenna laughs.

She takes a delicate bite and nods, agreeing. 'Mm, wonderful,' she says.

'Now,' she says, 'for the story.'

I continue eating, savouring every bite, while she speaks.

'My parents were both born to clans in the Ordovices tribe, in a hilly land far to the west of here. They were from different clans, but each of them chose, as they reached adulthood at fifteen, to become a druid and so travelled to the Isle of Mona to study. Druid training can take as long as twenty winters, but my parents didn't stay that long. They met a little way into their studies, fell in love and were married, but continued their studies a few more winters. After a while, the urge to travel and explore got the best of them, and they decided to set off from the island. They had gained a great deal of knowledge, and had a deep understanding of nature and the goodness nature can provide, but they couldn't reconcile this in their minds with what they had heard of human cruelty. Surely if nature was providing for people, then they could live happily and peacefully? But the stories they heard told otherwise, and they decided they needed to try and understand this for themselves, first-hand. They set off from the safety and security of the island – a beautiful, loving community – and went north to colder, harsher regions, staying with friendly clans as they travelled. Eventually they reached the sea and travelled down the coastline, finally coming to the land of the Iceni.'

Brenna pauses to enjoy another bite and let this part of the story sink in, then continues, 'It's at this time they met your father's parents – your grandparents – and they connected with these warm, generous people. They became very good friends and had a wonderful time together, enjoying deep conversations around the campfire with singing, dancing and music.'

'Your grandmother gave birth to Bellator shortly after my parents arrived, and then my mother fell pregnant with me. Mine was a difficult birth, and they wondered if she would make it through. My father was in absolute despair, thinking he had lost her. She survived in the end, but became so weak it was impossible she could ever make the long journey back home again. They decided to settle here, with this clan – your clan – and they were welcomed in as family. I was accepted as a child of the clan and raised as though we had always been here.'

'As your father and I grew, I worked hard to be respected in the clan. I wanted to be seen as my own person – capable and courageous – by my peers, and by the ruling warriors and elders. I wanted to gain their respect and friendship. In the end, this was an ideal position for taking over leadership, although that certainly wasn't my aim. I think it was just my history that made me work that much harder – I knew the clan hadn't needed to accept me in, and I felt grateful for both the family and the fact that my mother had survived her ordeal. I trained as a warrior and could hold my own, but I was not the best. There were, and still are, some truly great warriors among the group – Bellator being one of the very best – and some people wanted the strongest to rule. In the end, it was Bellator's vote that swayed the clan towards me.'

'I tell you this,' Brenna continues, 'because I want you to understand what a chief truly is. I can fight. But more importantly, I can rule. A chief must be the war leader, and see more than the individual – to put the group first. But a chief is also the clan's diplomat, and this is possibly the most important role of all. It's this way that a chief works to lessen her clan's need to fight, and pushes for peaceful resolutions to disputes.' She pauses. 'It is this way that I hope to fulfil my parent's desire – to work with nature to provide for all of us and fend off human cruelty.'

Brenna pours us both another mug of tea. 'For if everyone is provided for,' she says, 'and no one is going hungry, what right does anyone have to take from another or harm another? It's only power and greed that get in the way.'

My bread long gone, I take a sip of my tea thoughtfully. I understand what she's saying, and I think I agree with this. I can see how a peaceful resolution is favourable to violence.

'But aren't there times when this doesn't work?' I ask. 'When people won't work together or refuse to even try?'

'Of course,' she says, 'and this is why we train. For this we must be prepared. To defend our people, our children, our home. It's unfortunate, but there are still many clans who prefer this way of life. But we must continue our message of peace to them.'

Brenna finishes her bread and sets down her plate. 'Delicious,' she says and smiles at me. 'Did you enjoy that?'

'Oh, very much,' I say, 'thank you,' wondering if this is the end. I'm still not entirely sure why she has asked me here today…

'I've heard about the hunting challenge,' she continues, 'and your actions. I'm wondering how you feel about it.' I flush, embarrassed to talk about this with her so openly. 'It's okay,' she says reassuringly, 'I'm not here to judge you.'

'I…well, I…' I stumble over my words. 'I just think it proved that I can't be a leader.' Brenna looks surprised. 'A chief has to make difficult decisions,' I continue quickly, 'and surely it was more important that I catch the boar so the clan could be fed?'

'Aha,' says Brenna, 'I see where your thoughts have taken you. Let me ask you this – if no one had caught the boar, would the clan have starved?'

'Well, no,' I say, 'not right now. But that's only because it's the harvest…'

'Right,' she says, 'but even a couple of months from now. Could you have gone out again the next day?'

'I suppose so…' I say thoughtfully.

'You made the best decision for the situation you were in – the decision of compassion,' she says. 'You put the wellbeing of your competitor above the needs of your own pride and desire to win the challenge.'

'I just couldn't leave someone behind…' I say.

'Exactly,' says Brenna. 'And that's what is needed to be a great chief.'

The fire has burnt down to glowing embers now, so Brenna gets another log to add to it. I stare at the flying sparks, deep in thought.

'It's a different skill,' Brenna says quietly. I look at her.

'Strength, might, power – these are all needed to differing degrees depending on the situation. But the ability to put others before yourself, to make quick decisions that result in peaceful and healthy endings – this is the way to be a loved and respected chief, a chief who can help to change things for the better.'

I get shivers down my spine as she says this and look back at the fire to try and contain my emotions. A great chief…changing things for the better…these are powerful words – and a great responsibility.

'Have you had to make any sacrifices to be the chief you want to be?' I ask her.

Now she looks at the fire, suddenly saddened. 'That's a good question, Cara. Yes, in fact I have. Although I think perhaps anything you do of meaning in your life requires some sacrifices.'

'I know you think of me on my own,' Brenna continues, 'but I was in fact married once, a long time ago, before you were born. We loved each other a great deal and planned to live out our days together. But once I became chief it was different; he no longer saw me the same way. And he decided, when it came down to it, that he didn't want to feel "second" to his wife. Some of our most powerful leaders are women, and it's sad that he let my achievements make him feel less.'

She looks at me and says, 'It doesn't have to be like this. Many men don't feel this way at all, and the strong ones will support their wives in whatever they choose to do, just as strong women will support their husbands in whatever they choose to do. To follow your heart and do what you love – that's what makes you best able to love another person and want the best for them.'

'In any case,' she continues, 'it hasn't kept me from being happy – we are friends again now, and have been for a long time, and there are other men…perhaps someday I will find one I can put up with every day.'

We both laugh.

'However,' Brenna carries on, 'with no children of my own, I am looking to others for the future chief – when I'm no longer able to lead in the necessary ways. And, as you know, I am thinking of you.' I blush and look down quickly at my hands in my lap. 'I hope it will be many winters still, but it is something for you to think about, something to consider as you go about your training.'

Brenna pauses, and I look up to see her staring into the fire. 'We just never know…,' she says, 'if great battles erupt, well, anything can happen.'

She looks up to me and brightens, 'It is not, of course, up to me alone. But your actions will be remembered.' She pauses then smiles, 'And that is all I will say.'

She reaches out and clasps my hand. 'Do not be afraid, Carassouna. I have seen in you much to be proud of and I know you can do this if it's what you want. But there is no need to decide now. So, enjoy your training and enjoy your time to be young.'

Brenna lets go of my hand and sits back again. 'How are you finding it, settling back in to the clan?' she asks.

I'm hesitant to confide in her.

'It's okay,' she reassures me. 'Anything you tell me stays in the confidence of the chief's counsel.'

I am just bursting to talk to someone and it all pours out in a rush, 'It's just that there are so many different feelings, I don't know how to make sense of them all. Things are so much more complicated now, and my best friends since childhood have changed, or I've changed, or we've all changed – and are changing – and it's so hard to know how to feel.' I take a deep breathe, feeling like a wave has rushed through me, relieved to have these thoughts out in the open air.

'Senni,' I continue more slowly, 'has confided in me that she used to feel in my shadow, and wasn't at all happy, which I never even knew! She says she's overcome that now, in her time away, but how do I keep it from coming back? How do I make sure it's okay? And Drustan has mentioned how I couldn't possibly know how much he missed me – and he is definitely looking at me in a new way. But I feel differently about him as well. He was always like a big brother to me, and now…well, now my feelings are changing. It's all mixed up.'

'Carassouna,' Brenna smiles, her eyes and face lighting up, 'thank you for sharing this with me. This is all perfectly normal – most people go through an emotional upheaval at your age, and indeed for a few years to come, with changing feelings that are difficult to pin down. It sounds to me like you and Senni have set a great foundation for your future relationship just by talking about it.'

'And as for you and Drustan,' she winks at me. 'Well, I saw you dance together last night. There may be something more there – but as for what it is, you'll have to find out. You know our intentions for you; the tribal alliance may depend on you – but it may not. Nothing is certain. We all may have to make difficult decisions, and possibly sacrifices.'

Brenna rises and I stand up as well. She clasps both my hands in hers and looks straight at me. 'Do not be afraid, Cara,' she says. 'Everything will work out in its own time. Trust yourself and your instincts.'

As I walk home, I think about Brenna's humble beginnings here in the clan, and how she rose from an outsider to chief. I think of all that exists outside our clan, how I long to explore, to meet other people, but wonder if they are really any different from my family, my clan right here. We are all people, after all, and all dealing with the same feelings.

The sun is high in the sky now, and I feel hopeful for the future ahead. I have so much to think about.

Six

Later that day, I set off from the hillfort to visit the surrounding countryside. I walk past the animals in their paddocks, happily munching their way through the day. Such a peaceful existence for the most part, and so simple – I envy the simplicity of their lives in a way, with no need to make difficult decisions.

I continue on through the fields and see the farmers working, sweating in the late afternoon sun. We are in the midst of harvest – the farmers' most intensive work period of the year. They have hardly a moment to rest or sleep, working from sun up to sun down to get the crops in and sorted, some ready for use right away, most stored for future use. If they can't get enough food stored, or something happens to it once in storage, there is a real fear that people in the clan will starve.

The talk I've had with Brenna has made me think about

my future. I think I could do this. I think I could lead, but what about the other members of the clan? Would they even want me? And is it what I want for my life?

I head towards the wood to gather some herbs. I wonder about the herbal concoctions that our clan elders make to help heal the sick and injured – this is something I'd like to learn more about. There are so many herbs that can be used in different formulations, but it's very important to get it right – the way they're mixed together has the potential to change what would have been a healing potion into one that prolongs an illness.

I reach the wood and start searching. I've heard about a few new herbs being used, new ideas people are trying – I'd especially like to find these.

The sunlight filters through the trees as I gather the herbs in my wicker basket, and I enjoy the peace and solitude of this place. It's only a small wood but is a place I've come to since I was a child, seeking solace in the greenery and animals of the brush. The birds are active today, chirping and flitting from tree to tree, while creatures of the ground scuttle around, rustling leaves and breaking branches. The warm air surrounding me and the melodic birdsong help to focus my mind, and I settle into deep, thoughtful concentration.

A little while later, my basket loaded up with the fruits of my labour, I sit and lean back against a tall oak tree, satisfied, and just take it all in. I breathe in deeply, soaking up the lush, moist air of the wood.

Out of the corner of my eye, I see a little rabbit hopping towards me, then stop, sensing I may represent danger. Slowly, gently, I start humming a little tune, and the rabbit takes another tentative hop towards me. I wait a few moments, then carefully turn my body towards the rabbit and, unbelievably, it stays put. We stare at each other, its big brown eyes looking straight into my bright blue ones. The little nose twitches curiously, and I smile, wondering what it's thinking. Then a large scuffle off to my left breaks the still, quiet air between us, and the rabbit darts off, back to the safety of the brush.

The magical encounter fills me with wonder, and I feel lighter than air as I stand to go, dust myself off, and pick my way carefully through the brambles and out of the wood.

I wander back through the countryside, past the animals, the sun deep in the sky now – everyone and everything visibly enjoying a break from the beating sun of the day.

I reach the hill surrounding the fort, but for some reason I find myself walking straight past the entrance. I continue on, letting myself feel free in where I choose to go, then settle down to watch the sun set, colours already streaking the sky.

I set my basket down beside me and lie back, hands behind my head, thoughts swirling in time to the clouds passing by.

'Well, fancy seeing you here,' a familiar voice suddenly says from above.

My eyes jolt open. I didn't even realise I had closed them; I must have dozed off. Drustan's friendly face is smiling over me.

'Sleeping on the job, are we?' he says jokingly.

'How long have I been asleep?' I ask hurriedly, sitting up and wiping my eyes. I see the sun is only slightly lower in the sky – it couldn't have been that long.

'Well, I only just got here, so I don't know for sure,' he says, 'but you certainly looked peaceful.' He smiles again and sits down beside me, then looks at me seriously. 'How are you?' he asks. His face shows care and concern. 'I hear you've been at Brenna's house today? That must have been...interesting...' he adds wryly.

I blush, embarrassed, worried he'll sense how much I enjoyed feeling special. 'Oh yes, well...' I try to brush it off. 'It's nothing really, she just wanted to talk to me about the hunting challenge.'

'Oh?' he asks, eyebrows raised. 'What about it?'

'Well, just wondering about the details, that sort of thing,' I tell him, nonchalantly.

'Hmm,' he nods, staring off at the distant horizon. 'Was that all?'

'Ah, well...I suppose there were a few other things we talked about...' I pause, not sure how much I should reveal. Was that a private conversation? Who else knows about Brenna's history and her rise to chief? I look sideways at Drustan. He is my oldest friend. Surely if I can tell anyone, it's him…

'Well, to be honest with you…' I begin seriously. He instantly looks back at me, deep in concentration. 'I did feel honoured. She shared with me her past, details I never knew before. She made me feel…strong. In control. More in control than I actually am, probably,' I laugh, trying to ease some of the awkwardness of the conversation.

I choose my words carefully, then go on, 'I know some people expect things of me, and I know what's planned for me, but I also know I need to decide for myself. Brenna helped me see that I don't have to be the perfect warrior to be chief. Leading is so much more than that. I think maybe I could do it. I have a lot to think about,' I add.

Drustan smiles at me, wistfully. 'Carassouna, I know you could do it. You could do it better than any of us.' He looks away again. 'But I don't know what effect it will have on other things in your life.'

I think I know what he means. How many ways would my life be different if I were chief? I play with the blades of grass in between us thoughtfully. I can't imagine ever going without my two best friends again – I missed them so much when we were in fosterage. But where will they end up? I never thought of us being apart again; I thought we would either be here together or go exploring together…but what if they want different things?

I peek up at Drustan from the corner of my eye, his face in profile bathed in the warm glow of the setting sun. I notice that his golden hair is spiked with lime again, the spikes circling his head and streaks of white bleached throughout. He's been experimenting with lime more now, which the men of the tribes use often – especially when going into battle. I think about his future; I worry about him getting hurt, or worse. I can't bear to think about that, and impulsively reach out and touch his shoulder.

He looks over at me and smiles, then turns to face me, taking my hand in his. My heart flutters at his touch and the intensity of his gaze.

'Cara!' my mam's voice cuts sharply across whatever Drustan was going to say. I startle at the sound and snatch my hand away, then turn to see her walking towards us across the side of the hill.

'I thought you would have seen me waving!' she says exasperatedly when she finally reaches us.

Drustan and I hurry to apologise, saying at the same time, 'Sorry mam' and 'Sorry lady Vendi.'

Mam looks at us suspiciously.

'We were just watching the sunset,' I say, motioning to the now almost-dark sky ahead of us, 'coming back from gathering.'

She looks from my basket of herbs to Drustan's basket

of fish. Suddenly a bat swoops down over us and we all jump.

'Well I've been looking for you, young lady,' she chastises. 'You didn't tell me you were going to be out until tomorrow! Let's get inside now.'

And guiding us both towards the gate, we walk home in silence, whatever Drustan was about to tell me left unsaid.

SEVEN

'Just a little bit more….and stop. Stop!' I hear Lucilia say, her voice rising in volume.

I look over to see her and Mato at the baking table nestled near the side of the roundhouse. A huge cloud of flour dust has just filled the air around their heads.

'Oh, Mato,' Lucilia says, 'what a mess!'

'Sorry,' Mato's little voice says sadly.

'What are we going to do with all of this?!' she exclaims.

'Sorry!' he says again, his lower lip trembling.

'Just be more careful next time!' she chastises him harshly.

He bursts into tears, wailing 'I'm sorry!' over the din.

I hurry over and see a great pile of flour spread across the table and onto the floor.

'Oh Mato,' I say and sweep him up in my arms. 'Lucilia didn't mean to make you sad, she's just worried about wasting food. Don't worry though, it's okay,' I say to him and rock him back and forth in my arms, kissing his head.

For the past few days, I've felt as though I'm floating dreamily through life. My magical day in the forest and on the hillside with Drustan is all I can think about, filling my thoughts when they are supposed to be elsewhere. Sometimes growing up is difficult and complicated, but not that day. What was he going to tell me? My mind wanders through the possibilities.

I love the summer, the sun and the heat, but today that's broken as the rain lashes down outside our cozy roundhouse. The worst of the storm seems to have just passed by, with its booming thunder and huge streaks of light in the sky. I peeked out from between the big double doors until it seemed much too close for comfort. I think everyone's on edge, which would explain Lucilia losing her temper when she's normally so patient. But now the noise is quieter, and the booms are much further apart – it's moving away from us.

The farmers have called a halt to the harvest for the moment; the conditions make everything take so much longer, and the risk of lightning strike is too great in the open fields. They've also been busy moving the animals in from pasture, closer to the houses in the farmsteads.

Little Mato, not enjoying being stuck indoors, asked to learn how to make bread. This honour fell to Lucilia, who was rather reluctantly instructing him on turning a few ingredients into one of our main food staples.

I'm experimenting with some of the herbs I gathered in the woods – some still fresh and soft, some which I've dried by the fire. I can see my little pot smoking and smell a rather revolting stench coming our way.

'Eww,' I say without thinking, then look down at Mato. He's stopped crying, his nose wrinkling in disgust as the smell reaches his nostrils. 'Let me get that out of here,' I say and put him down next to me on the bench.

I hurry over and grab the cloth holder, take the pot off its iron hangar, and rush it outside. When I open the door, a wave of moist air hits me and I see the water streaming in sheets from our roof. That should take care of the smell fairly quickly. I duck out from the safety of the house, place the pot in the stream of water and dart back into shelter – soaked after only a few seconds.

I come back inside and close the door firmly behind me, then feel a strong hand push it open straight away again.

'Not so fast, my dear,' a deep voice says.

My father appears, followed closely by my mother and several others. Their heads are buried deep in their cloaks as they scurry in from the relentless rain.

'Ah, what a day!' exclaims my mother, pulling off her cloak and brushing herself dry. 'Here, let's get your things dry,' she says to their friends, gathering cloaks.

As they uncover their heads and my eyes adjust back

to the dim light with the door closed, I recognise many of my parents' closest friends: some farmers whom they work with tirelessly to ensure we all have enough food; others warrior friends who fight side-by-side with my father.

'Morning to you, Cara,' my mam's best friend says to me, coming up and putting her arm around me.

'Morning, Gleva,' I say, and give her a hug.

It's interesting to me that despite their separation, she and Mam have stayed closer than ever. I think it's their strong relationship that helps our hillfort thrive.

'Oh, Mato! I forgot!' I exclaim and rush back over to make sure he's okay.

Mato seems to be past it and is busy mixing the flour with water and a pinch of salt. Lucilia glances up at me.

'I'm really sorry,' she says, 'I know I overreacted.'

'It's okay – I know you were just worried,' I say to her.

'Thanks,' she smiles at me and I smile in return.

Gleva comes over and puts her arm around Lucilia, speaking to her about the plans for her fosterage. Lucilia's face lights up with delight, and I'm so happy for her.

With everyone settled back in, I return to my herbs and try to remember the quantities I had put in that pot… where did I go wrong?

The adults have gathered round the fire warming themselves, while Mam puts a pot of water over the fire to boil and hangs a pot of stew somewhat further away to gently heat. The benches look fuller than I expected; I hadn't noticed quite so many people coming in from the rain. But now that I see everyone sitting together, I notice it's quite a distinguished gathering, with most of the prominent leaders of our clan, save Brenna. I wonder why she's missing, but Tad interrupts my thoughts.

'Cara, can you please help me serve our friends?' He brings over a tray of cheese and bread, which I take from him and walk around the group serving. Mam pulls the boiling water from over the fire and infuses it with mint leaves, leaving it to rest and reach a rich, dark green.

Meanwhile, Tad gathers mugs and bowls from the shelves near the wall and brings them over. Mam ladles a spoonful of the scented, warming liquid into each mug, which I hand out.

'Thank you, Cara,' Tad says, and their friends echo his thanks. I take this as my cue to leave the group, so with a nod excuse myself and return to my herb table.

Lucilia comes over to chop some rosemary, leaving Mato pounding and kneading the bread. 'Why do you think they're here?' she whispers to me over the table, not looking up from her work.

'I don't know,' I whisper back truthfully.

'Do you think there's something…bad?' she whispers, looking up at me furtively. I shrug. I wonder if we should be worried?

I try to get absorbed back into my work as I hear the

adults discussing crop rotation and how to ensure the soil has the best nutrients for growing different types of food. That doesn't sound too ominous to me – maybe it's just the rain that has driven them all in here, an opportunity to chat and eat together.

I return my attention to the herbs. I know I mixed one part of these leaves and one part of those roots with a pinch of ground meadow sweet. I'm trying to make a salve that helps cuts heal more quickly, using a recipe I was given by one of the clan's elders. I wonder if I'm missing something? Or perhaps put too much of something in? I'm sure it shouldn't smell that bad! I think I'll start again and see if I just made a mistake. I lay out the herbs on the table, trying to make sure I've identified each one correctly.

The adult conversation hums along in the background until I hear a heated debate rise up over the best recipe for hops beer. Lucilia and I look at each other and smile, then she returns to help Mato shape his bread and start baking.

My hands move deftly; I enjoy this work with herbs and plants. I smell each one and try to imagine how they will smell when combined, the best scent combinations. We can use plants for so many things – healing, dyes, flavouring our food, scenting the air – they are so versatile. I find it really amazing.

The adults are now enjoying the stew that Mam heated, and she brings bowls over for me, Lucilia and

Mato while we work. From the drone of conversation, I hear the words 'tribal meeting' and my ears prick up. A tribal meeting is an extremely important occasion – it happens only once per season – when representatives from across the entire Iceni tribe gather. The chiefs of the clans use these meetings to discuss concerns and make big decisions, drawing on the experience and wisdom of the elders. I listen more carefully now.

'…and they have not shown respect,' one of the clan warriors is saying. 'They mustn't be allowed to gain any more power.'

'Well how do you expect us to stop them?' another warrior chimes in. 'We can't actually forbid them to continue building up their forts and villages. Even if we did, how could we possibly enforce it?'

'It is of utmost concern to us all,' my father concedes, 'and this is why we will have the meeting with the Trinovantes.'

The Trinovantes? This is a big deal. I can't resist…

'What meeting with the Trinovantes?' I ask, walking over to the group seated around the fire.

My father smiles a bit, but my mother is not happy, 'Carassouna, you are not yet an adult; this isn't your concern.'

'Now then, Alauna,' says my father. 'We're not with-holding information from the clan. Cara is just curious; she has a right to know what might be of great impact on her life.' Mam does not look happy with that answer; I think she would much rather I stayed a child forever.

'Cara,' Tad continues, the attention of the group now riveted on him and me. 'We're expecting a visit from the Trinovantes tribe. They're sending a group of their clan warriors and any elders who can make the journey for an important discussion about Catuvellauni's growing power and wealth. As we both share a border with them, it is of great...' he hesitates, '...concern. And we think it's best if we work together on this.'

Of course, I have already heard about this.

'What might they do?' I ask.

'What wouldn't they do is the question,' the farmer on my right pipes up eagerly.

'That's enough,' my father says firmly. 'We don't know,' he answers me. 'No one knows. We are only concerned of the possibilities; we think it's best to discuss them together. We are stronger together,' he adds.

'So,' another warrior pipes up, 'we've been chosen to host the visitors, have we not, Bellator?'

'Yes, that is true,' my father replies. 'It is a great honour. And very unusual for a clan so far on the outskirts of tribal land. But we're a peaceful clan, and it's thought we are good representatives of the outlook of the Iceni tribe.'

My mind is spinning; this is huge news. How long have they known? When will this happen? Who will come? Where will they stay?

Then another thought crosses my mind, a thought which is almost more disturbing than the thought of tribal conflict – I wonder if this honour is due in any part to my fosterage with the Trinovantes? I know the idea was to strengthen ties between the tribes…what if Gavo comes to the meeting? What if I have to make a decision soon…perhaps very soon?

I feel my cheeks burning. The continuing conversation seems a distant din, as though I'm surrounded in a fog. Why have they put this pressure on me? Why can't this just be my choice?

I suddenly notice that Mam is staring at me strangely, so I try to push these thoughts out of my head and give her a weak smile. I don't know how much they've noticed my head in the clouds over the past few days, or if they have any idea why, but I'm certainly not going to share my feelings with them now – not with so much at stake.

EIGHT

The day of the tribal meeting dawns, and I wake suddenly to hear unfamiliar voices drifting in from the main area of our house. Surprised, I sit bolt upright, worried that something's wrong. Then I hear the reassuring sounds of my mother laughing and Mato squealing in delight, and flop back in bed, trying to slow my pounding heart.

This must be the first of our visitors, arrived already. Has the sun even come up, I wonder, thinking I will just go back to sleep. I roll over and bury myself in my blankets, closing my eyes against the noise. But my head has already started working – I remember why I'm so worried about today. What if he's here? Will my eyes give away my true feelings? And what is expected of me?

Grudgingly, I push back the blankets and force myself out of bed. At least it's not too cold this morning, so I can dress at my own pace. Autumn is settling in, but today it seems a return to the warmth of summer.

I put on my best tunic – blue, of course – and sit down at my dressing table to bead my hair and put on my ornaments. My mother and Senni always like their hair braided, as do many women of the clan, but I prefer mine loose. I love the feel of it on my shoulders and the weight of it when I turn my head, the way it falls in my eyes or across my face sometimes, and especially the feeling of the breeze blowing it back when I ride Morna across the fields. Besides, I don't think I can really be bothered to spend that much time on my hair; it takes so long to braid it properly.

Instead I string through some glass beads. We're lucky to have these; many clans can't afford them. I install my ornaments – bracelets, armband and gold torc around my neck – and grab my cloak in case the morning air is brisk.

I have a quick look in the mirror. There, that should be presentable enough for a special day like today. I take a deep breath and gather my confidence to face the day, whatever it may bring.

As I part the curtains around my sleeping area, I find a crowd of strangers sitting around the fire eating breakfast – there must be ten or twelve at least! It feels a bit peculiar knowing there were so many people sitting near me while I was getting ready. Sometimes a curtain doesn't feel very private.

Mam hurries over looking apologetic. 'Oh Cara, my dear, you look surprised,' she says, and I nod. 'I'm so sorry, I think I may have forgotten to tell you we'd be having some guests for breakfast today…' I nod again.

My mother, always strong but graceful, today looks absolutely majestic in a gorgeous, green flowing gown almost sweeping the floor, tied with a brown tasselled belt around the waist. She is always one for ornaments and face painting, and today she has outdone herself. Even her hair appears brilliant, glowing with seemingly hundreds of beads woven into her three braids, which themselves are braided together.

She takes me by the arm and leads me over to the guests, a mixture of stately, confident and impressive women and men. She makes the introductions all around and informs me that these are all fellow tribespeople, leaders of the Iceni, who've arrived early for the day's events so that they might have some time with Brenna and the clan warrior leaders before the Trinovantes representatives arrive. As it turns out, only four of them will be sleeping in our house, while the rest – all clan chiefs – will be staying with Brenna.

'How did you get here so early?' I ask.

My voice must give away my surprise, because many of them laugh. One of them, a grey-haired, distinguished-looking woman I believe my mother introduced as a clan chief, gives me a warm smile and explains that they had

103

all arrived at nearby Wighton the day before, so as not to put us out an extra night while still arriving here early. Their thoughtfulness makes me feel more at ease, and I welcome them all to our home. My mother looks pleased with my graciousness.

'If you'll excuse me please,' I say, 'I'll just have some breakfast with the children.'

'They're just outside,' my mother says, and I welcome the excuse to head out into the fresh morning air.

As I step out, I can see the sky is a clear, bright blue and cloudless – brilliant in the strengthening sunlight. I wonder if the children are hiding and walk around the outside of our roundhouse to the back, where I find them sitting on the ground with breakfast on their laps.

Smiling, I sit down next to Lucilia and say, 'Let me hide with you.' She smiles, and Mato laughs. I enjoy sharing a secret with my brother and sister; we've come a long way since I arrived home, and are so much more comfortable together now.

I break off some bread and cheese, and Lucilia hands me an egg, still warm. We silently enjoy our food together, a moment of peace before a day of action.

When we're finished, I take them out to the common area to see what's going on. The hillfort is a flurry of activity this morning, with noise and people everywhere. I see Senni and wave her over.

'Hi!' she says brightly. 'Are you just out?'

'Well, sort of,' I reply, sharing a secret smile with my siblings.

'There's so much to do,' she says. 'The Iceni leaders have been arriving already, since just after dawn, and they're all being put up in houses. The Trinovantes are being given the meeting house for sleeping – they say there are thirty-six people coming! And more than fifty from the other Iceni clans…it's the biggest thing we've ever hosted.'

'What should we do?' I ask her.

'Hmm..' she says, distracted by a sudden shout from near the stables. I see a tall boy waving her over. 'Sorry, I've got to go,' she says. 'We have to move all of the animals out of the stables – except the horses, of course – so there's more room for visiting horses.'

'I'd better check on Morna,' I say, almost to myself, then remember my siblings are with me. 'Let's go visit Morna,' I say to them cheerfully, 'then we'll find some jobs to do.'

At the stables, Morna is a bit distressed by all the commotion.

'There, there, girl,' I say soothingly to her. Lucilia and Mato stroke her side while I fetch her some treats – a carrot and an apple should make her feel happier. 'I know, girl,' I whisper to her. 'I'm sorry we can't go out today – there's too much to do. I promise we'll go out tomorrow.'

'We're just going to take the horses out to pasture

for a while,' the stable hand says to me, coming up with Drustan's horse already on the lead. 'Don't worry – we'll make sure they're put back in their own stable blocks, not moved around by all the visitors.'

'Thank you,' I say to him appreciatively. 'Let me know if you need me at all.'

Lucilia, Mato and I move on as he takes Morna's lead, and I pat her side as she walks by me. She shakes her head up and down in response, with a little whinny; I expect she's happy to be leaving all this chaos – time for some nice green grass.

We head back towards home, thinking I will ask Mam what she needs help with. People pass us with arms of firewood, heading towards the main fire pit in the common area. Others are moving benches into the space, creating a larger fire circle, while still more people decorate the space to prepare for dancing. Musicians are setting up off to one side, and I happily see my favourite instrument, the lyre. That sweet sound was playing the night Drustan and I danced for hours.

Off to the other side, we see barrel upon barrel of different types of ales surrounding the granary. The first barrel is tapped and tested by the ale keeper, a respected and well-placed woman of the clan.

Once past the common area, I can see beds being assembled in a little space between houses, on the opposite side of the path from our house. Hay and straw is stuffed inside cloth sacks, which are stitched up to form a makeshift bed – just fine for a night or two when laid on the floor.

I've never seen so much activity in the hillfort. Little Mato looks around with his mouth wide open, and Lucilia appears entranced as well.

I laugh, 'It certainly is exciting. I feel a bit useless though. Shall we see what we can do?'

Nodding they follow me back to our house, where we find my mother busying herself laying out the extra beds and covering them with blankets.

'Oh good, you're back,' she says. 'We've been given the beds, but I think we need a few extra blankets. And your father asked if you could go out and get some honey?'

'Father? Where is he?' I ask.

'He's already gone into Brenna's,' she replies. 'All the Iceni leaders have arrived. They're in meeting now probably until the Trinovantes arrive.' That explains why the doors to her roundhouse were closed when we walked past.

'Where should I look for extra blankets?' I ask her. What a boring job. She looks at me, exasperated.

'I'm sure you can figure that out, Cara,' she says and continues with her work.

Lucilia offers to stay behind and help Mam prepare the food she's bringing to the feast, so just Mato and I set back off, bringing the honey glove with us. I have no idea where to go for blankets, and just wander aimlessly, holding his little hand. He willingly follows wherever I go. We end up back near the stables again, and I turn the corner of the last roundhouse to find myself face to face with Drustan.

'Oh!' I say, surprised.

He looks startled, but pleased.

'Cara,' he says, 'and Mato,' looking down. 'How are you, little chap,' he asks, lifting Mato up easily and tossing him in the air. Mato laughs happily.

When Mato's safely caught again, Drustan says to me meaningfully, 'I've been thinking about you.'

Even though I try to stop it, I feel heat rush into my cheeks. Not wanting to admit he's been occupying my thoughts, I just say, 'Hmm,' and look away.

'Where are you two off to now?' he asks.

'We've been told to track down extra blankets,' I roll my eyes, 'and also get some honey.'

'Honey?' Drustan asks, surprised. 'With Mato?'

'Who knows what Mam is thinking?' I say. 'She's a bit distracted.'

Drustan nods his head knowingly. 'Well, let me come with you. The last I heard, the hives were pretty full and I wouldn't think it's very safe for little ones.'

Impressed by his thoughtfulness, I thank him and we set off on the honey mission – out of the hillfort and around the back, where groups of little hill-shaped willow baskets are dotted across the field, surrounded by wildflowers.

Drustan carries Mato on his shoulders and sings as we walk. As we come around the side of the fort, he explains to Mato how the beekeeping works. 'You see the baskets over there, Mato?' he asks. 'Those encourage the bees to settle and make honey.'

'Does it work?' asks Mato.

'Well, for the most part they're pretty successful,' Drustan says. 'That's how we're able to get so much honey to put in our food and drinks.'

'Mm, sweet honey,' says Mato. 'Yum, yum.' He licks his lips, and Drustan and I both laugh.

'It is pretty good, Mato – I agree,' I tell him.

Once we're close, but still at a safe distance, Drustan takes Mato down from his shoulders and tells us to wait here, then carefully heads towards the first group of hives. The bees aren't very happy to have their honey taken away, so this can be a dangerous job; it's good of Drustan to want Mato to be safe.

He heads towards the hive furthest away from us and peeks in through one of the doors on the side. Apparently happy with what he sees, he puts the honey glove on and sticks his hand in – the hole in the plaited willow made just big enough for a hand. I can see him grimacing, even from here. He quickly pulls his hand back out again – and he has some comb! He repeats the exercise on a second hive, then a third, then returns to us with his booty, dripping with the sweet, golden liquid.

Mato is delighted and asks for some straight away, so Drustan breaks off a little piece and gives it to him, then holds the rest out for me.

'For you, m'lady,' he says with a playful bow.

Smiling I take the honeycombs from his hand. I break off a piece and give it to him, then have a bit myself. The gooey, sticky-sweet goodness coats my teeth and then my throat sliding down, and I feel an instant rush of happiness. I spit out the wax left behind.

'Thank you, Drustan,' I say to him. 'Is your hand okay?' I ask, reaching out for his gloved hand. 'It looked like that first one hurt quite a bit.'

'I think you have a hole in there somewhere,' he says, 'I definitely got stung.'

'Let's have a look at it,' I say to him, pulling the glove off. I can see the padding under his thumb is red and swollen with what looks like more than one sting.

'Let's get back home,' I say, 'I have a tincture that will take down the swelling.'

'Don't worry, I've had worse,' he says, but I insist, and we set off quickly back towards home.

A new group of visitors is arriving just as we get to the entrance, so we try to slip past without too much notice.

At home, Mam greets us with, 'Oh good Cara, you're finally back.' I roll my eyes while I'm turned away from her. 'I don't see any blankets? Well never mind, I've had some brought to me anyway, so I think we're fine now.'

She hurries on, 'Good to see you Drustan, how are you?'

'Very well, thank you, lady Vendi,' he says, bowing slightly to her. He always knows just what to do, I think to myself, looking on impressed as my mother seems pleasingly placated.

'Drustan's hand has been stung,' I say, heading towards my herb store to get the ingredients I need.

'Oh dear!' my mother says, rushing to him and lifting his hand delicately. 'Oh, it looks quite bad,' she says. 'Cara was meant to be getting the honey,' she says accusingly. 'What happened?'

'Well, we ran into Drustan on our way and he offered to get it for me. Because I had Mato with me,' I add hurriedly.

'Oh, right,' says my mother. 'Well, that was very kind of you, Drustan. I'm sure Cara can patch you right up; she's getting quite good at these things.'

'Thank you,' he says, and Mam heads off with Mato on some other job.

I bring my supplies over, and as I get close he says in a low voice, 'I have no doubt about that.'

I pretend not to hear him.

'Here, let me see your hand,' I say to him brusquely.

We sit down on a bench by the fire and I examine his

hand in the light coming in from the doorway.

'You're even more beautiful when your mam's telling you off,' he says, and I look up to see him smiling at me. I can feel the heat rising in my cheeks again and am mad at my body for betraying me.

Trying to focus, I lean over his hand, intently applying the tincture I've mixed to the swollen areas and checking for stingers.

'I only see one stinger,' I say to him, 'but we'll have to get it out.' I take out the numbing agent I've brought over and rub it gently over the area then get the small tongs ready. I'll have to really push in to get it out and I know it's going to hurt, numbing agent or not. I lean close to get a good look at it and can feel him leaning his face down near my head, brushing against my hair with his cheek. I try to concentrate and focus on getting a good grip with the tongs. And…I brace myself…

'I'm not interrupting anything here, am I?' my father's voice booms.

I pull.

'Aaahh!' Drustan cries out, trying to jerk his hand away.

'Got it,' I say triumphantly, holding the stinger up between the tongs.

'Drustan was stung,' I say to my father. 'Getting honey for us,' I add.

'Aha, I see,' my father says, a hint of uncertainty in his voice. 'Hmm, well, sorry to hear that Drustan. And good job, Cara, for getting that stinger out – you don't want an infection.'

He continues, 'Our meeting is done, and the Trinovantes have just arrived at the entrance gates. I'm here to get your mother and everyone; any idea where she's gone?'

'I'm sure she'll be back in a minute, Tad,' I say. 'She was just busy getting things ready, like everyone.'

'I'd better go,' Drustan says, standing up hurriedly. 'Thank you, Cara. I'll see you both outside – Cara, sir,' he bows slightly towards me and then my father, then rushes out.

My father watches him go with a troubled look on his face, then looks at me. I look down and gather up my things to put them away in the herb store.

'Cara, you and Drustan – you have grown up like brother and sister. And I am very fond of him, you know I am. But…' he pauses. I busy myself putting things away, my back to him. 'These things are not always our own to decide. Sometimes we must do what's for the good of the group, the good of the clan.'

I don't want to hear what he's saying and try to drown him out with my own thoughts. I don't care what he says, I will choose my life.

But today is not the day for an argument. I wonder how to avoid it, when Mam saves the day, bustling in with Lucilia and Mato in tow.

'Oh good, you're done,' she says to father. 'Just in time – the Trinovantes are here.' He rolls his eyes secretly and all of us children laugh.

'Yes,' he says, 'that's just what I've come to tell you.' He smiles and gives her a kiss on the cheek.

'Excellent,' she says and takes off the smock protecting her best dress, then smooths down the skirt. 'I think we're ready.'

We walk as a family to the common area, where our clan is gathering on one side. The other Iceni leaders are gathering opposite and the Trinovantes are being led into the space between, forming a triangle shape with Brenna standing in the middle. My mam and tad move towards the front of our clan with the most prominent adults, as is the custom, while the children, teens and other adults stand behind the leaders. The musicians I saw earlier stand off to one side, instruments poised and ready.

I scan the Trinovantes group quickly for signs of Gavo and am relieved to see he's not among them. Sadly, neither are my foster mother or father – I was hoping I might see them here.

Once everyone has arrived, Brenna begins to speak. 'Welcome, our friends, our guests. It is a great honour to have you all here today with us. We have here,' she gestures towards the other Iceni leaders, 'gathered a group of our most esteemed tribal leaders, who have brought the Iceni tribe to great prominence: chiefs, warrior leaders and elders. All are welcome. And over here,' she gestures towards the Trinovantes, 'it is our great honour as an Iceni people to welcome the esteemed leaders of the Trinovantes tribe: your chiefs, warrior leaders and the elders who were able to make the trip. We understand that some of you have been travelling as long as four days to reach us here today, and for that we are very grateful. I will not keep you long; I promise we have much food and drink prepared for you now, and a great feast planned for this evening.' Many in the crowd chuckle at this, and I am again in awe of how well Brenna takes control of a crowd, making all feel comfortable and welcome.

'These are serious times we are living in,' Brenna continues, 'and there are serious discussions we need to have. Many may threaten our peace and our security. But in all times of seriousness, we must also remember to feel grateful for what we have, to appreciate the bounty of our land and the joy of the company of family and friends, both old and new. And so, let us first enjoy being together and make merry.'

'We present to you, our friends of the Trinovantes, a cape of our colours, blue and gold.' One of the warrior leaders walks forward, holding in his outstretched arms a beautifully woven cape. 'May you long remember your time with the clan of Warham fondly. We also present an iron shield, forged by our beloved blacksmith.' The blacksmith joins the warrior leader in the middle of the triangle, holding the shield out. 'Long may this last as a decoration, as together we seek to find peace.'

The Trinovantes leader steps forward to meet these two in the centre. 'Chief Brenna, on behalf of the Trinovantes people, I gratefully receive your gifts and thank you for your gracious welcome. May our tribes live together in peace forevermore, and may we work together to find peace with others. We look forward to our time here with you, and hope to repay the favour to your people.' He bows and accepts the gifts given to him, then the crowds assembled break into applause.

'And now,' says Brenna, 'let the drink flow and the music play!'

A huge cheer erupts from the crowd, and instantly the musicians begin, right on cue. The crowds disperse, with people moving every which way, and I grab hold of Lucilia and Mato's hands to keep them near to me. With close to two hundred people filling the common area, it seems a very busy place – and easy to get separated. We seek out Mam and Tad to find out what to do next.

Tad sees us coming and gestures us over to them. 'Now, this is a very special occasion, as you know,' he says when we reach them. 'There is much to do, so it's your job – with all the children and teens – to bring out the food and pass it around. Make sure our guests are happy. Some of the adults will be finishing the feast preparations; others will be speaking with our guests.'

'Well done, all of you,' Mam says, and gives us all a squeeze, then sets off for the main cook house while Tad goes to join Brenna speaking with the Trinovantes leaders.

I see the tables set up near the granary, next to the barrels of ale, and steer us in that direction. Luckily, Senni is already there and we agree that her sister and Mato are a bit young for all of this.

'You stay here and...make sure the trays stay full,' I tell them. Mato and Minervina giggle and run off to play. I don't mind, there isn't really much for them to do.

Senni, Lucilia and I each grab a tray and head off into the crowd to find some hungry people.

The musicians have built up speed quickly and already people are dancing, letting loose and enjoying the spirit of the day.

When I return to the table to refill my tray, Senni is already back and looking worried. 'What's wrong?' I ask her, concerned.

'I don't know...' she trails off, looking around nervously. 'I don't know if this is important.'

'What is it?' I ask. 'You can tell me.'

She lowers her voice and says, 'I've just heard that some of the Iceni clan representatives are missing. There isn't anyone here from Hunstanton...or Thornham.' Thornham, the place of her fosterage. 'Why would that be, Cara?' she asks. 'Do you think that's something to worry about?'

'I don't know,' I say honestly. 'I don't think so…'

But something about that doesn't feel right, and I can understand why she's worried. Why would you miss the most important event for your tribe, especially when you live so near to where it's happening?

'Are you still in touch with anyone there?' I ask.

'No,' she says, 'I haven't been back to visit yet, and the last time someone from Thornham came here, they were gone again before I even knew it.'

The ale keeper bustles over to us, loaded down with cups and mugs. 'That's enough you two,' she says, 'there's too much to do for you to stand around chit-chatting. Cara, will you go ask your mam how long until the feast is ready? I'm going through the ale barrels at quite a pace; I think people will need some hearty food in them soon.'

The sun is low in the sky already, as the days shorten with the passing into autumn. I'm sure the children are hungry too, so I hurry to the cook house and find Mam along with many other men and women surrounded by vats of food and stacks of bowls, spoons and knives.

'Oh Cara,' she says, 'brilliant. The feast is ready; can you please tell Brenna?'

I turn around, wondering how I became the messenger, and set off to find Brenna, spotting Mato and Minervina on my way.

'Dinner time!' I say to them, and they cheerfully follow me. I whisper the news to Brenna when I find her, then go to select spots on the benches for the little ones to eat.

Brenna makes the announcement, and everyone quickly finds a seat: outside, if they can, enjoying the warm evening air, or in the meeting house sitting around the fire.

Of course, it's my job to serve as well, so I resign myself to hunger and shuttle bowls of stew back and forth between the cook house and the benches, both outside and inside. There are twelve of us serving, the "children and teens" of the clan, but it feels like it takes hours to get everyone their food. When I finally sit down, darkness has fallen, but Senni, Drustan and I find a place by the fire and enjoy our food quickly, sure that Brenna is going to announce the meeting any minute.

Mam tells me she's taking Mato and Lucilia home, and I say goodnight to them just as Brenna stands up on one of the benches nearest the musicians to get everyone's attention. They finish their song and play a little jingle to announce Brenna. She thanks everyone involved for the delicious feast and announces that the meeting will begin now in the meeting house.

I finish my stew and think I'll head home, as my friends are. It has been an exhausting day and I feel really tired, ready for my bed. Brenna appears at my side as I stand up.

'I hope you'll be joining us in the meeting house, Cara,' she says.

'Oh,' I reply, surprised. 'Me?' I ask.

She laughs, 'Yes, we would very much like to have you there.' I wonder who 'we' is.

'Okay,' I say, a bit unsure, but she vanishes as quickly as she appeared.

My friends have already made their way back to the cook house, so I'll have to go on without saying goodbye. I'm sure they won't worry about me, just think I was too tired and had to get to bed. I'm not sure I want to see them right now anyway…I'm guessing they weren't invited to the meeting house…

I need to hurry; I don't want to walk in late to that.

I arrive at the meeting house just as they're closing the giant double doors. Relieved, I take up a spot near the door, back against the wall. Seating arrangements are always by priority, with the leader seated in the centre of the ring, in her own chair, facing the door. Brenna sits here now, looking majestic in her dark red gown, with her long jet black hair swept up to one side and pinned in place. The light from the flames illuminates her face, and she is the most beautiful, strong figure I have ever seen.

Circled around the fire, on the benches to her left and right, are the most prominent leaders of the Iceni and Trinovantes tribes, the groups intermixing as I suspect Brenna arranged them. The elders of the tribes have priority even over the chiefs, as the wisdom and experience they've gained in their age is respected and esteemed over power and strength. There are two rows of benches tonight, such are the numbers at this special meeting. Standing behind the benches are clan warriors and less prominent leaders, and behind them are the leaders in training – namely me.

'Before we begin,' Brenna says, 'let us listen to the bards, as they share with us some of the great poems of the Iceni people, many created by those who left us long ago.'

Three bards stand up, each in a different area of the roundhouse, and they take turns reciting poetry – regaling us with the rhythmic lyrics telling the history of our people, accompanied by the lyre. The group is silent as they listen, taking in the beautiful language and the feeling of the words, the fire crackling in the centre of the house and casting shadowy light all the way out to the edges, where I stand.

I am getting cold now and envy the warmth of those sitting close to the fire. I can see beads of sweat on some of them even, and I pull my cloak closer, hugging myself for warmth. I can feel a chill of air coming in through the cracks of the doors.

When the bards have finished, they quickly leave and Brenna turns the meeting straight to business. 'We have assembled,' she says, 'not in fear, but in preparation. The Catuvellauni tribe are building their wealth and power – more than ever before. Many of us are concerned at what they will try to do with this; where it will lead. Do we trust the leaders? Can we be sure they won't try to expand their boundaries? Take over our lands? These are some of the important questions we need to discuss tonight and over the next day or so.'

As she is speaking, I hear faint sounds outside, coming through the door, where before there was only silence. Is that the bards? Am I imagining it? I look around to see if anyone else can hear anything, but they are all listening intently to Brenna.

Thinking I must be imagining it, I move slightly away from the door, trying to get a little closer to the fire without being closer than I'm allowed. But the sounds outside seem to grow louder even though no one else gives any indication they hear them. I start to panic, worry taking hold as I definitely hear shouting. I look to Brenna, and she suddenly seems to hear it as well, surprise registering in her eyes.

She stops speaking, and people look around at each other, startled. Still the thundering sound of fists pounding urgently on the door takes me by surprise and makes me jump, sounding as though a giant is trying to break through.

I feel a tremble run through my body with the uncertainty of what lies beyond that door, and wish I was anywhere but next to it.

NINE

Brenna keeps her composure and walks towards the door, followed closely by Tad and a few others. I try to trust in the guards who are keeping watch at the entrance this night. Warriors throughout the meeting house are on their feet now, their hands on their sword hilts.

She opens the door nearest me, and I can see through the crack a small group of people; one of our guards is nearest me. I breathe a slight sigh of relief.

'It's Hunstanton,' he says to her, trying to catch his breath, 'at the gate.'

I can't see her face behind the door, but instantly the rest of the house is on its feet, surging towards the doors. I slip out, trying to stay close behind Tad, and follow the crowd moving quickly towards the entrance gates.

The guards have let them in, as they are a small party, and they're gathered in a staunch huddle just inside the entrance, the gates open behind them. Their faces are painted in dark blue woad, as if prepared for battle.

As Brenna approaches at the front of the crowd, one of the group steps forward, his hand outstretched before him.

'Chief Brenna,' he says stonily, 'I see the rumours are true; we have been insulted.' She starts to speak, but he cuts her off quickly, angrily, 'Not to invite us here tonight, to a tribal meeting? You will pay for this injustice.'

My mind is racing…not invited?

The clan of Hunstanton are an important fishing and trading port, more central to our tribe than Warham. I knew there were problems sometimes, they could be very difficult…but this is serious. My heart sinks as I remember the clan of Thornham is also apparently missing; the clan where Senni fostered, for whom she has such strong feelings and cares so greatly. I wonder now if they were invited…

I can't see Brenna's face, but I can see her back stiffen as she raises herself to her full height. My father's face is difficult to read; I can see the muscles tightening in his jaw.

A voice calls out from the Hunstanton group, 'The clan of Warham should take great care – we will be back. This is not the end.'

Around me, many of the warriors make a move to ready their weapons, but Brenna simply answers back,

'This, my fellow Iceni, is not the time nor the way in which to handle this situation.'

'My warriors, stand down,' she says to the people around her. 'We can reach a peaceful resolution.'

The Hunstanton warriors erupt in jeering laughter at this statement, and Brenna's face tightens, yet she retains her composure.

'You are a woman,' the leader speaks out again. 'We understand you want to save face in front of your fellow tribespeople. This is why you always call for peace.'

'In fact,' she says in return, 'I invite you to join us here in the meeting.'

A stunned silence follows. I don't think anyone expected that. I am astounded by her confidence in the face of these intruders.

'No, we won't stay,' their leader finally answers.

'Very well then,' Brenna says, 'we will escort you out.' She motions to my father and some of the others to see them out. 'Know that my door is open to you; we are allies, not enemies. Ask your chief if he will come, with his council, in two days to meet with us,' she says.

My father and the other warrior leaders move towards the Hunstanton group.

'We'll be back,' their leader says ominously as they are led away from the hillfort, going without a struggle for now. Back when, I wonder? To the meeting...or before?

Once they are out of sight, chatter erupts from every

direction, breaking the tense silence. Brenna turns to face the gathered crowd and eventually brings back their attention.

'I think we will call an end to the meeting for tonight,' she announces. 'Don't worry, we will meet again tomorrow. Everyone could use a good night's sleep. Thank you.'

People return to their conversations, slightly more subdued, and the crowd begins to disperse. I feel both relieved and worried: nothing like this has ever happened in the Iceni tribe as far as I know, where a nearby clan has threatened a chief so publicly.

The kindly older woman who ate breakfast in my house this morning must see me looking concerned, because I suddenly find her at my side telling me not to worry. 'We are in good hands, my dear,' she says, looking over at Brenna. 'The best. Come now, let us gather the group for your house and you can lead them back.'

TEN

In the light of day, things always seem less sinister.

We are all back in the meeting house now, having slept (or barely slept, in my case), breakfasted and regathered to pick up where we left off.

With so many guests sleeping in our house last night, I found it full of unfamiliar noises, different breathing patterns and snores, lots of rolling around. My mind was wide awake and active despite my body feeling in desperate need for rest, and it was quite close to dawn by the time I finally slept.

I am still in shock, still can hardly believe what happened last night. Why weren't the Hunstanton clan invited? What were they going to do now? My home had been intruded upon, threatened, and I didn't really feel safe anymore.

Brenna is now in the midst of her meeting. She's

reviewed the reconnaissance collected on the Catuvellauni, gathered by various scouts from each of the tribes. The mounting evidence seems to suggest they are a force to be reckoned with – and a force that may try to take our lands. There is no longer any doubt in my mind that we need to form an alliance with the Trinovantes – we simply aren't strong enough to take them on alone. And that leads us to…

'…the clans of Hunstanton and Thornham,' Brenna declares. 'Some of you will be aware why they were not invited to this meeting, but for those of you who are not – I apologise for keeping you in the dark. This will help you to understand why: the Iceni tribal leaders have reason to believe that these two clans are working with the Catuvellauni.'

Brenna pauses, and the meeting house erupts in an explosion of voices at this earth-shattering news. My stomach drops and time seems to slow down, the voices surrounding me muffled into background noise as thoughts go racing through my head. How could this be? Not Thornham – Senni's beloved foster home? Surely, they couldn't be involved in something like this?

Now she holds her hands up for silence and gradually the meeting house comes back to order.

'This is not definite. This is what we suspect, what may be happening. We just couldn't risk inviting them and giving away our plan if it turns out they are in collusion.

What we do know is that members of the Catuvellauni tribe have been reported in the area more frequently recently. Some of them have been tracked directly to Hunstanton where they were welcomed in. They didn't appear to be traders, only travelling in pairs and without carts of goods. But we do not know who they are or why they were there – they didn't register as visitors at Thetford, as is the custom.'

One of the Iceni elders speaks up, 'I would give them more credit than that. If they really were visiting for unscrupulous reasons, wouldn't they go disguised as traders? I think we may be over-reacting...'

'Well, we can't be too safe with what we're planning,' my father replies. 'Any inkling the Catuvellauni get of an alliance forming may cause them to attack before we're ready.'

A Trinovantes leader stands and addresses the group calmly, 'To me, this just reinforces what we were already thinking – that we don't have enough information.'

Brenna nods, and moves to stand next to him, addressing the group again, 'Agreed. This is what we've all been saying today – we don't know enough. We must be prepared, but for what? We propose putting together a joint travelling group to visit the Catuvellauni lands – a dangerous task for those involved, but one that will bring us back more information on which to build a solid plan.'

There are nods throughout the room, as people look

around at each other, seemingly in agreement. I wonder if I should volunteer? It's a chance for adventure, although it will almost certainly be the older, more experienced warriors who are chosen for this mission.

The leaders agree that this group must set off very soon, before the Catuvellauni have the chance to find out about our alliance or make a move against us.

Brenna continues, 'I propose that this group meet just inside the Trinovantes' land, where the three tribal lands meet. They will need to go into the Catuvellauni's land on the new moon, so they have about ten days to prepare,' she says. 'Each tribe will choose two people to go on this mission; we will choose carefully, considering the stealth, knowledge and experience needed. Do the leaders agree to this proposal?'

There are nods and 'ayes' all around, although it fills me with dread. To sneak into their land, under cover of night, is so dangerous.

I hear Brenna announce that the meeting is concluded. The Trinovantes will be leaving, in order that they are gone before the meeting with Hunstanton; a few of the Iceni tribal leaders will stay to deal with them together.

All the leaders stand to go, and I find myself standing up as well. The kindly woman from last night comes over and puts her arm around me.

'You have done well,' she says to me quietly. 'It is not an easy road ahead for you, but I can tell you will handle it with courage and grace.' She squeezes my shoulder then turns away. I feel a shiver run down my spine – as if her words have sunk to my very core. I realise that I still don't know her name, still have no idea who she is, and turn to run after her – but she's disappeared.

My father and the other clan warriors are in front of the fire now, talking with Brenna in low tones as the visiting leaders prepare to leave. Brenna motions me over.

'Can you sound the horn?' she asks. 'We need to see the Trinovantes travellers off.'

I find the carved, curved horn near the door of the meeting house and take it outside, feeling honoured as this is the first time I've been asked to do this. I put the narrow mouthpiece to my lips and blow – but nothing comes out except air. I try a few more times and finally get a shaky sound…I take a deep breath and follow this quickly with a loud, short burst. That will have to do. Then I call – 'the Trinovantes are departing' – and immediately my fellow clanspeople stop what they're doing, come out of their houses and gather around the entrance gates to the hillfort. Brenna and the clan warriors stand outside the meeting house, embracing each visiting guest – as is the custom – as they exit the meeting house and move towards the gates.

Most of the other Iceni leaders are also preparing to leave and take their turns bidding farewell to my clan's leaders. As Drustan finds me and comes over to say hello,

I am distracted in seeing the kindly woman again – she looks at me, smiles and nods elegantly.

'Who is she?' I say, almost to myself, under my breath. Drustan follows my gaze and sees the woman.

'Oh, that's Vinda,' he says. I look at him in disbelief. 'She's chief of the Caistor St Edmund clan,' he continues, unphased. Drustan knows her – this is where he spent his fosterage.

'Do you know much about her?' I ask, hoping.

'A little bit,' he says, 'I know that she's a Druid, which is a very unusual background for a chief. But there's something about her…'

I look at her, transfixed, wondering – but my thoughts are broken by the cheers of the crowd, as the leaders are now gathered at the gates and waving farewell.

We wave them out of the hillfort and out of sight, then the crowd disperses quickly – back to their daily work, back to normality. Brenna takes the remaining Iceni leaders back into the meeting house and I follow, eager to hear more about the plan.

They waste no time in agreeing a way forward. The clans weren't invited because there were reports that they hadn't contributed their fair share for Lughnasa, our harvest festival.

'It's easy enough to explain,' one of the tribal leaders argues. 'There are different levels of contribution, and we received information that they hadn't met their required level. We tell them we needed to discuss this together to agree what should happen, but we've investigated and find only a minor infraction.'

'I like this idea,' one of the other leaders chimes in. 'It also provides us with a reason for this meeting – why we needed to meet again, so soon after Lughnasa. I think we should offer a conciliatory gesture as well, perhaps that they will host the next tribal gathering. This should help appease their injured pride.'

The leaders seem in agreement, nodding to one another.

'And what of Thornham?' Bellator asks, and the nodding stops. Silence.

Brenna speaks up, 'Well, I don't think there is much we can do about Thornham at the moment. Perhaps they don't even know about the meeting?'

'That's true,' the first tribal leader agrees. 'We don't really know how Hunstanton found out, and possibly they aren't in much communication with Thornham.'

'Is everyone in agreement?' Brenna asks and again there is nodding around the room.

'Excellent,' she continues. 'Then we will break the meeting here and assemble again once Hunstanton arrive tomorrow. The tribal leaders will continue to stay with me until that time. And thank you for remaining to help us with this,' she says to them.

I leave the meeting house and run straight into

Drustan. A sudden urge to ease my conscience and reveal all that I have learnt overwhelms me, but I know this isn't possible. The success of a mission like this depends upon as few people as possible knowing. Not that I don't trust Drustan – I do absolutely. But suppose someone were to overhear us? I can't take that chance, but can't think of anything else to talk about.

'I'm really sorry, I've got to check on Morna,' I say hurriedly and rush away before he can offer to come with me. I try to push out of my mind the confused expression on his face.

I head towards Morna but then secretly double back and make a quick stop at my house. An idea is forming in my mind – a way in which I might save Senni the pain and sorrow I feel is coming her way. Or not; it all depends on what I find out. But either way, knowing is better than not knowing. The house is thankfully empty for the moment, so I quickly grab my bow, quiver and arrows, hiding them under my thick, woollen cloak. I also find a small hunting knife that my father gave me as a child and I tuck this in my belt for safekeeping.

When I arrive at the stables, Morna is munching away on hay. 'Come on, girl,' I say to her, stroking her neck and patting her side, 'let's get out of here.'

'Where are you going?' a voice asks innocently from behind me.

I turn to see Senni looking at me in surprise, her eyes

134

moving back and forth between my face and my quiver and bow slung over my shoulder. I realise I'm going to have to tell her something.

'I'm going out to investigate,' I say honestly. 'There's been some news at the meeting today and I just want to see what I can find out.'

'Is it about Thornham?' she asks, her eyes giving away her concern. I had hoped she wouldn't ask.

'It's Hunstanton,' I reply, which is the truth – even if not the whole truth. She doesn't look convinced. I need to persuade her.

'It's important. Please,' I say imploringly. 'You have to trust me – I can't tell you why right now, but I will as soon as I can.'

'But what if it's dangerous?' Senni asks, concern on her face.

I feel so grateful for my caring friend, I smile and hug her. 'I can't just sit here and do nothing,' I say with a sigh, pulling back to hold her shoulders and look into her eyes. 'I'm so sorry I can't tell you all of the details. Please help me.'

She nods grudgingly, and I quickly finish getting Morna ready before she can change her mind.

'Cover for me, okay?' I say to her as I pick up my things again. 'I'm on horses today, so as long as you're here, no one will even notice I'm gone. I'll be back this afternoon.'

I give her one more quick hug and squeeze her arm with a smile. 'Thank you.' Then I quickly lead Morna out of the stables without looking back.

We walk across the hillfort, taking the back way behind the houses. I keep a steady pace, restraining myself from running straight out of the gates. When we finally get through them and start down the hillside, I climb on to her back. Suddenly I am yearning for freedom, longing for it – to be outside the hillfort, away from the suspicion and fear.

'Yah!' I say emphatically, giving a nudge with my heels. We take off galloping, turning south then heading west again. I know where I want to go, but I'm not sure I should.

We leave the hillfort behind quickly and it's soon out of sight. After a couple of minutes at full-out gallop, I slow Morna down to rest with a gentle walk while I think.

The tribal leaders are definitely suspicious of both clans, and it makes sense: their position near the end of the Peddars Way would make it easy for the Catuvellauni to get there and back without attracting too much attention – the trail ends right in between the two clans' lands. And that trail connects to the Icknield Way, which I've heard runs all the way to another sea. Who knows how many tribes live in between?

I find myself thinking these are things I really must learn if I'm to become a chief.

If the clans are working with the Catuvellauni, they might also be working together. And if they are, there must be some sign of it. That's what I need to look for.

Morna looks back at me with one eye then swings her head forward again, asking me if we're ready to go. I know we're a morning's ride away at a good pace, so I give her neck a rub.

'Good girl,' I say to her. 'We'll go to the Peddars Way. Let's see what we can find there.'

I nudge Morna on with my heels and she breaks into a steady, lolloping gait. I adjust my position on her, holding more tightly with my knees. At this pace, she can go on for leagues, as long as I stop for water from time to time. It's harder on us both, but we need to travel quickly.

It does cross my mind that they might have guards on watch. What if I'm captured? I need to stay alert.

Without thinking, my left hand moves to the pouch at my waist. Here, deep within the folds of cloth, my magic amulet is buried in amongst other treasures and tools.

Every person carries a pouch and an amulet. Mine is deep golden amber in the shape of a teardrop. My grandmam found this piece whilst on the coast during her fosterage, mixed amongst the shingle on the beach. She passed it to my mam when she was starting her journey to the spirit world, just before I was born. Mam was certain it was meant to be, that this would be my amulet.

I've kept this piece of amber in my pouch since I was

old enough to wear one. I feel it now – a solid, reassuring presence – and carry on.

Almost there now, I smell the salty sea air as we near the shoreline. I have to pass Thornham to reach the Peddars Way trail, and the settlement there is very close to the sea. I wonder if I can get a look at it from the other direction – the seaward side? I decide it's worth a try.

Morna and I take a detour on a small path that opens out onto a riverbed. We follow this, seeing the sea ahead of us, and are north-east of Thornham when we come to an inlet, the river mouth flowing quickly into the sea. I see tall dunes surrounding us to the west; I'll climb up there to look out at Thornham.

Feeling sheltered and isolated, I leave my quiver and walk along the sand, marvelling at the difference of this seashore to the salt marshes near Warham. Here, the ground is covered with golden grains, sparkling when the clouds part to reveal the midday sun.

I take off my shoes and walk barefoot, feeling it sift between my toes. I stop and cover my feet, amazed at how cold it is so near to the surface – although the sun has warmed those surface grains, the ones not two thumbs below feel as frosty as night.

Seashells peek up from the ground and I pick one up,

turning it over in my hand to admire the smooth under-side of its swirls. I tuck it in the pouch at my waist – a treasure to save for later.

This close now to the clan homes of Hunstanton and Thornham, but strangely I feel better than I have since last night's events. Somehow facing my fear relieves the severity of it, lightens my heart. I begin to feel brave again, the way I felt when I was in the meeting house and out by the gates. I know that I would do anything for my family, my clan and my home. Anything to protect the people and place I love so dearly.

It's funny how one can want to leave and at the same time feel so attached to a place. The yearning to travel and explore, to be different to my mother – and yet, at the same time, the strong force drawing me back home.

Morna has wandered over to eat the grass on the dunes nearby, so I join her to climb this lookout. Once at the top I can see for leagues, but the trees are tall and vast between here and Thornham. I spot what I think is the top of their settlement, but I can't be sure.

Not wanting to be spotted, I hurry back down and Morna and I continue our journey, moving back to the main path. As we near Thornham the trees thin out, but we pick out a trail that keeps us close to the woodland as we make our way through the gorse-covered hills.

The walls of the settlement suddenly appear as we crest the next rise, and I quickly dismount and step into the cover of trees. Not really a hillfort, as there's no great hill here, the clanspeople of Thornham have built a settlement enclosure with very high walls. Watchtowers guard the entrance on the inland side, but they have a more open presence on the seaward side. Primarily a fishing people, their settlement leads directly to the estuary and their lives are run by the tides.

I hide in the trees now as I observe the watchtowers. The massive entrance gates are huge wooden constructions. I see a glimpse of guards in the watchtowers and hope to remain undetected. I guide Morna stealthily through the trees that run parallel to the south, making as little noise as possible and staying back from the treeline.

As we move across, I notice some sort of flag raised from the western tower – a white cloth fluttering in the breeze. I haven't seen this on a settlement before. Could it be a signal?

Past the settlement and feeling safer again, I think I'll move Morna back to the main path as soon as we crest the next rise and are hidden from view. But just before, some sense tells me to turn back, and I see a person step through a small gap in the western wall – then the gap disappears.

I blink. That can't be. I stare at the spot and urge my eyes to focus at this distance. I can see a faint outline of a gate – a place where the palisade boards are a slightly different colour than the rest. It's as if someone hastily knocked out part of the wall and then had to repair it – only now it opens. It's very convenient that this camouflaged entrance faces the Peddars Way – and Hunstanton.

Finally past Thornham, the trees thicken again as the shoreline moves further out. Morna and I keep a quick pace through here, keen to reach the trail now that we're so close. Approaching from the south, I can see the break in the woods ahead, then emerge into open space. My breath catches in my throat as I take in the view.

With the woodland cleared, I can see for leagues down the path to the south – it appears to go on forever, disappearing over the horizon. I wonder how many have walked this path before me? Certainly the Catuvellauni could quickly and easily make it all the way here.

I also see the woods on either side and wonder who could be lurking there? A chill runs down my spine and I feel the hairs on my neck stand up as I realise I am all alone and very exposed.

On cue, Morna gives a whinny and shakes her head, as if to remind me she's still here – I'm not completely alone. 'I'm glad you're here too, Morna,' I say as I rub her neck and give her a quick pat. 'Let's head this way.' I turn her towards the north.

We trot up the path as I examine the surroundings for clues. What the tribal leaders didn't discuss much at the meeting is that trade with any Iceni clan has to go through the tribal centre at Thetford. In fact, any visitor from outside the tribe should stop in to register their presence. Knowing the recent travellers haven't been doing this makes it more likely they are a threat.

I can see up ahead a willow statue standing at a fork – a giant fish with its mouth pointing down the path that leads to the sea. The lefthand fork – a smaller path – should lead directly to Hunstanton. This is why they feel so superior; they really are a critical tribe for our people's connection to other lands. I can understand that they feel they should be hosting tribal meetings.

The distant sound of thudding hoofs reaches my ears and my heart jumps into my throat. Sudden panic grips me and I look frantically back on the trail but can't see past the last bend. Quickly, I slide off Morna and lead her down the path towards Hunstanton, then into the trees.

We crunch through broken branches and undergrowth as quickly as we can to get back off the path, then I pull her to a stop as the hoofbeats get closer. Nuzzling my face into her neck, I whisper to be quiet and she answers a soft grunt, holding still and calm while her big brown eyes show her care and concern.

The noise gets louder until suddenly it seems to stop almost directly across from where we stand hidden, back on the main path. I catch my breath and can feel my heartbeat pounding in my ears. Have they seen us? Do I dare peek around Morna to check?

I hear voices – talking to each other, not yelling in

my direction – and take a chance that they're not looking this way. I slowly peer out from under Morna's head and can see three riders on the path, now dismounted from their horses. They seem to be discussing which way to go, pointing in different directions. Eventually the tallest one leads the way down the path to the sea, but they don't disappear from sight right away. The last horse and rider linger in my view and I wonder what they're doing – are they being left behind as watch?

Finally they too are gone. I wait a few minutes to give them time to get further down the path, and to make sure no one reappears. Morna and I slowly and quietly move back to the nearest path, but I don't mount her yet; instead we walk stealthily towards the intersection as I hold my breath, my heart feeling like it will jump right out of my chest.

I peek around the trees lining the path – and see nothing. No one. It's as if they've vanished into thin air. The next bend is far off in the distance; there's no way they could have made it that far.

My head pounds as I try to make sense of this. Could I have imagined them? They were definitely real to my senses – I could see them, hear them, feel the vibrations in the ground as they galloped up the path. Is it possible to imagine something so vividly?

I walk forward hesitantly, gripping Morna's lead tightly as if my lifeline to reality. I look around at the trees surrounding the path and down at the very ground itself, wondering if they've been swallowed up inside. Shaking my head, I know there must be a reasonable explanation.

The only place to hide here is the trees. Looking left and right, I slowly walk down the path, still trying to be as silent as possible in case they're nearby. After awhile I give up – I just can't find any sign of them – and decide to turn around.

Almost all the way back to the intersection, something catches my eye in the bush to the left. I turn to look, and it's gone. Then again, something. This time I don't turn but try to see it in my peripheral vision. A gleam; a glint.

Bronze. I try to burn its placement into my eye then edge towards the side of the path. As I get closer to the bush, I can see just barely sticking out, resting on a branch, a bronze brooch. It must have been snagged in the thorns.

Looking up and into the trees beyond, I almost can't believe what I'm seeing – it's another path. Narrow and winding, it snakes its way through the trees. I realise this bush is the only thing blocking the entrance and look more closely.

There I see it – it's a door. Willow branches are wound around the trees to the left and right of the 'bush' – which is itself just the leaves of the willow. I look underneath; sure enough, no trunk – it's suspended in the air. I gasp with surprise and awe at the clever disguise, but my delight quickly turns to fear and sadness as I realise what this means, where this path must lead.

The Peddars Way runs directly between Hunstanton and Thornham. To the left is Hunstanton. Straight on is the sea. This path leads to the right – to Thornham. What reasons could they have for needing a secret, hidden path? No good ones that I can think of; Senni will be devastated.

I'm torn – I don't know what to do. Follow the path? It's dangerous, and the risk of discovery is great. Take the real path to Thornham? Then I'll have no proof that this secret one actually leads there. I'll have to follow it and see.

I move aside the doors and lead Morna through, though she shakes her head and sidesteps nervously with a soft whinny.

'Shhh, it's okay girl,' I whisper softly, stroking her neck and urging her forward. I decide that it's best if we're ready to run, so once through the gate – with it carefully closed and sealed again – I remount my close, trusted friend and we start down the path.

The woods here is thick and dark, with hardly any sunlight penetrating the thick canopy overhead. The path is intensely narrow to fit between the close-set trees and heavy undergrowth, twisting and turning, the lines of the trees playing tricks on my eyes so I lose all sense of direction.

I start to panic and Morna must sense my nervousness, looking back at me startled and alert. Once again I feel for my amulet safe in my pouch and grip it tightly with one hand, Morna with the other. I don't dare let her move more quickly than a walk for fear of making noise, but I remain on edge, ready to break into a run at any moment.

After what feels like a lifetime, I sense the brightening ahead and then finally see light beyond the forest.

I dismount and tie Morna's rope to the nearest tree so I can quickly run forward and check what's here. As I near the edge of the woods, I can clearly see the Thornham settlement. What's more, that secret door is directly across the field from where I stand.

ELEVEN

Once I've confirmed my suspicions, Morna and I quickly make our way back down the secret path. The longer we're here, the greater our chance of being discovered. We arrive at the main path, re-seal the secret willow door, and head back towards the known Thornham path.

So close to the sea the weather is very changeable, and thick clouds have gathered while we were in the woods, turning the sky grey and overcast.

I'm still keen to stay hidden while passing the settlement – certainly a young girl on her own will arouse suspicion. Rather than remain exposed, we'll dip back into the trees as we pass.

All is going well – we move back to cover just before we crest the rise that makes us visible to Thornham and move quietly through the trees past the settlement.

Feeling secure, I break cover a bit too early; a shout makes me startle and I turn to see a guard looking my way.

I quickly re-mount Morna and urge her into a full gallop. I realise this makes me seem guilty, but I'm here without permission and must avoid confrontation.

The moist, fresh air from the sea feels thick around me and I taste the saltiness as we ride quickly into it. A low mist has risen, floating above the ground, and I will Morna to meld into it; to blend grey on grey. I don't know how I'll get out of this one and reach instinctively for the amulet in my pouch. Even though it's just a stone, it makes me feel like I'm surrounded in a protective shield.

As we gallop over crest and trough, we cover the ground quickly and there is only silence behind us. I gather my courage to look back, but the path is empty. It could be a false security, so I urge Morna on again, putting ground between us and trouble.

I finally know it's enough when she slows to a walk of her own free will and looks back at me with her calm, steady eye. I quickly slide down from her back, lead her off the path into the trees and give her a huge hug around her silky, strong neck.

We walk through the trees, moving away from the main path. If we can get to the countryside, we can find a smaller path or even make our own way through the fields. We both need water, and food if we can find it. Moving through the undergrowth quickly, no longer needing stealth, we walk for a long time before we sense open space beyond the trees ahead.

Escaping finally, I step into the clearing and see the beautiful countryside before me, the mist near the sea having burnt off with the sun's re-emergence. The gentle rise and fall of the green land before us; the immense, fluffy white clouds brushing the tops of the hills in the distance; the deep cerulean blue sky. I stop to drink in the view and feel my body relax as I sense we are past danger.

I don't even want to think what could have happened if they had caught up with me. Just that thought makes me glance back nervously into the forest, but nothing appears out of place and only the birds and small creatures can be heard stirring.

Tired after our long day and eager to keep moving, I lead Morna off towards a brook in the distance, in the valley beyond. There are thick hedges that will keep us concealed while we drink.

It doesn't disappoint, with brambles covering the hedges, trees and bushes that line the brook. The blackberries are at their peak now, and Morna and I devour them eagerly, the delicious sweet-tart juice sticking to our lips and hands as we eat our fill. She eats them more quickly than I can pick them, so eventually I encourage her, laughing, towards the brook itself to take a drink.

My mind wanders back home. Brenna invited them back in two days – that's only tomorrow, but it seems like a lifetime away. I feel almost certain about Thornham now; I don't know how I'll face Senni.

As these thoughts swirl around my head, Morna and I set off from the brook towards home. Refreshed from our stop, she seems ready to ride so I remount; it's getting late and it's a long way home.

We cover the ground at pace, stopping only a few times briefly to walk and have a drink. As I near the hillfort, the setting sun is streaking the sky behind us in a brilliant display of red, orange and purple. I can't help stop and face the sunset, a last glimpse of the horizon I just travelled through.

Dusk is settling in when I finally make it through the entrance gates. I'm greeted by Senni and Drustan approaching me at a run, concerned looks on their faces.

'Where have you been?' Senni bursts out as she reaches me. 'We've been so worried about you!' she exclaims, throwing her arms around me.

Drustan stands back slightly, a hurt look on his face. 'Why didn't you tell us you were going out all day?' he asks. 'You wouldn't believe the stories we've had to tell for you.'

He stares at me and I feel a sudden pang of guilt for being so secretive. 'I'll go get you some water,' he mumbles, shaking his head, and skulks off.

'Come on', says Senni in a friendly tone, putting her arm over my shoulder. 'Let's get Morna bedded in for the night.'

At the stables, Senni quietly works with me to brush Morna down, not asking any questions.

Finally, breaking the silence, I say, 'I'm sorry – I didn't mean to worry you.'

She smiles in my direction, 'It's okay,' she says, 'we just didn't know what happened to you. We didn't think you'd be gone all day. Once the sun started going down, we worried you were in trouble or needed help, but had no idea where you were – or what was going on.'

Drustan arrives at the stables then, and I feel a now-familiar flutter in my heart.

'I'm so sorry,' I say to him. 'I really didn't mean to make you worry.' He looks somewhat appeased and comes to wrap his arm around my shoulder.

'Just don't do it again, okay?' he says gruffly.

I nod, although I realise even now – that's a difficult promise to make.

The work done, we sit down on the stable benches as I try to explain why I needed to be out, without giving too much away. They seem wary; I think they know it's not the whole truth.

'But you didn't go near Hunstanton, did you?' Drustan asks as I finish my story.

'Not too near,' I reply. He seems relieved.

Senni has a far-off look in her eyes as I talk about my time on the beach, and I can see them starting to fill with tears.

'Senni, what's wrong?' I ask, concerned.

She wipes her eyes hurriedly, laughing. 'Oh, nothing, it's just silly,' she says. 'I just really miss that seaside, the view, the sand.'

'Sand?' I ask.

'That's what they call the "grains" you were talking about,' she tells me.

'Oh!' I say surprised, and we all laugh.

'Well, it is beautiful,' I agree. 'So different to the oozing muck of the salt marshes.'

'You both must show me some day,' Drustan says and we agree to take a trip there together once this has passed.

We all stand up, and I'm happy to be feeling so much closer to them again. They both seem happy and relaxed as well.

'Let's take a walk,' I say impulsively. They look at me, surprised. 'I'm just not ready to go home yet, I feel so full of energy,' I say.

Shrugging, Senni looks at Drustan then back at me and says, 'Where to?'

I grin. 'Let's try the walkway,' I say, referring to the protected path that runs around the entire fort, just behind the wooden palisade.

Drustan smiles at me. 'Now don't get any ideas,' he says, 'we don't want you to fly up to the moon just yet.'

'Not today,' I reassure him, jokingly.

We climb up to the path, and I immediately feel transported. From here, we have an uninterrupted view of the surrounding countryside, and the bright sky feels so close I could reach out and touch an endless expanse of stars. The moon is waning, just a crescent tonight, and the low light somehow illuminates the grass and trees with an iridescent purple light.

As we follow the path around the north side of the hillfort, I realise we're nearing the spot where I first felt my heart flutter when Drustan held my hand. I wonder if he's feeling the same and look over at him. I need to find the courage to speak with him about it.

Senni steps off the path in front and motions us to follow, her finger on her lips signalling silence. Drustan and I follow wordlessly and creep down, trying to find where she's disappeared to, when suddenly she reappears grinning, holding out a loaf of bread. 'I forgot I had this earlier – I'd put it down for later. Well, now is definitely later!'

We all laugh and sit down near the large oak barrels of beer left over from the tribal gathering to share in the bread.

'Mm, that is exactly what I needed,' I say, 'I've hardly eaten anything all day!'

'Sorry I don't have anything to go with it,' she says thoughtfully.

'Oh no,' I say, 'this really is perfect.' I feel so lucky to have my friends.

Happy and satiated, I lean back and close my eyes, listening to the two of them joking around. Drustan learnt a load of silly rhymes and riddles from his fosterage clan – it seems their bard especially liked to make people laugh – and proceeds to entertain us with them.

After a while, I open my eyes and remember the glorious starry sky. I climb back to the walkway to admire it more closely.

I look straight up, feeling like I'm in the sky myself, until it starts to spin. Shaking off the dizziness, I come back to normal height. My eyes take in the huge expanse of sky over the fields and then turn to the woods. There's something about the trees in moonlight, they always look slightly foreboding.

As I turn away, looking back towards the fields, something catches my eye in the wood, and I instinctively duck slightly. What was that? I look again and see only trees. I look more closely, willing my eyes to sharpen and focus.

Nothing. I guess it was nothing.

Suddenly I see a flash of silver, and I duck down quickly behind the palisade.

My heart races and my body feels frozen. Could it be? I feel a hollow pit in my stomach, and suddenly I'm more certain than I have ever been of anything.

This is it. This is what I've been dreading.

They are just beyond the hillfort, hidden deep within the trees. I can feel it.

I peer through the gaps between the wooden ramparts. Thin clouds cover the moon, but when they break, the light again illuminates a glint of metal – and I know for certain.

'Cara,' Drustan's voice whispers from behind me.

I lower myself from the platform, willing my body to move noiselessly, and crawl on hands and knees towards them. Drustan waves to me slightly from between the barrels and I make my way over, careful not to move too quickly and draw attention to my position. Some of the gaps in the palisade are too large; I can't take any chances.

I make it behind the barrels and try to breathe deeply to calm myself. Drustan and Senni are both crouched here; they must have realised something was wrong when I ducked down so quickly.

'What's happened?' Drustan asks, his voice a hoarse whisper as it chokes with worry.

'There's something out there,' I whisper, 'in the woods. I think it's them.'

I look from Drustan to Senni, whose face is set bravely but whose eyes give away her true feelings.

'We have to wake Brenna,' I say quietly, 'I don't think we have much time, but she'll know what to do.'

As I speak, I hear a whinny come from the stables. Has there been a movement from the woods? Can the horses sense their presence? The air feels thick and tense, ready to erupt at any moment.

I motion for my friends to follow me. Deftly, quietly, we creep along the backs of the granaries until we reach the end. To get to Brenna's roundhouse, we have to cross the main path and common space – an open area of fifty feet. 'Wait here,' I whisper.

Staring at the space before me, I try to summon those feelings of bravery I had earlier. I try to think of how I feel when I'm riding Morna – free. Or when I met with Brenna – confident. I have to do this alone.

I gather my strength, and move quietly and quickly across the open common area, crouching low instinctively.

When I reach Brenna's doorway, I take a deep breath and let my racing heart slow down, but I can't stop to think about me – our whole clan is in danger. I creep through the roundhouse, past the fire and into her sleeping area – separated by those thick red curtains – then over to the bed where Brenna lies asleep. I kneel beside her and gently shake her awake.

'Brenna, wake up. It's Cara,' I whisper, leaning my head near hers.

She opens her eyes and looks at me sleepily.

'They're here,' I say.

And that's all it takes. It's time to fight.

TWELVE

'Night raids,' Brenna whispers to me as she pulls on her shoes, belt and cloak as quickly as she can. Her long black hair flows loose around her face and gives it the appearance of glowing, floating in the darkness. 'They don't often erupt into battle; it's usually the cattle they go for. But sometimes they'll try to enter the hillfort.'

She leans close to my face, her hand on my shoulder. 'Let's hope this isn't one of those times.'

As noiselessly as possible, we creep to her weapons store where she pulls out two swords. One she hands to me. 'You are ready,' she says. Then we softly pad out of her roundhouse.

'Wake your father up quickly,' she tells me. 'I'll get the others. We have to gather as many people as possible before sounding the alarm; once that goes, any element of surprise is lost.'

I crouch low and hurry into my family's house, never before quite so glad of our proximity to Brenna's house and the sheltered little courtyard we surround. My father has always been a light sleeper, and I find he is half awake by the time I've entered their sleeping area and moved to his side of the bed.

'Cara, is it them?' he asks, seeming to know why I'm here. I nod, and he springs into action.

'Brenna's waking the others,' I tell him.

'Where are they now?' he asks.

'They are – or they were – in the woods, northwest of the hillfort. I saw the glint of metal in the moonlight,' I add. He looks up at me but doesn't stop to ask what I was doing, or why I was still up.

'Let's go,' he says.

My father wakes my mother to warn her while I quickly go into my sleeping area and swap Brenna's sword for my new one – it seems the thing to do. We leave our roundhouse and see Brenna and six others assembled.

We gather in the little space between our houses, moving towards the common area, then spot another group moving across that space – Senni and Drustan have woken others.

I smile to myself at their bravery and foresight – I'm not sure I would have thought to do that – once again proud to call them my best friends.

Brenna must feel we've gathered enough warriors,

because she signals for all of us with her – and those across the common area – to meet at the stables. Crouching low and weaving between buildings, we make our way as two separate groups to the space at the east end of the hillfort where our horses are kept. On this side of the hillfort, opposite the entrance – and the woods where I spotted the raiders – the bank is steeper and we all feel more secure.

There's no time to prepare a chariot, but we quickly and quietly ready our horses and mount them, moving into formation ready to gallop down the path at top speed.

Up until now, everything has happened too quickly for me to think or feel anything. But now, with a moment to prepare, I realise just how terrified I am.

The other group has gathered shields and distribute them now; Drustan helps pass them out. Our eyes meet as he hands me one, and all our feelings are conveyed with one look.

In what seems like not enough time to gather my thoughts, we are ready. My father makes a gentle but distinct bird call to warn the guards at the entrance gate, and we wait for their reply. It comes back shortly.

That's all we need.

Vastini – I only just spot him with us – takes the war horn down from the wall, an honour for a junior warrior.

'When we pass the gates,' Brenna says to him. Then to all of us, 'Ready?' I find myself nodding in return. 'Let's go - hya!' she cries.

We charge – straight ahead across the path, through the entrance gates which have been flung open by the ready guards, and along the zigzagged entry. As we pass through, Vastini puts the horn to his lips and an incredible, deep, elemental sound rings out through the night air.

From a little way off, we hear confused shouts.

'The paddocks!' Brenna calls out, leading the charge. I'm amazed she's able to pinpoint the location of the sound; I wonder how she can do this. Unquestioningly, we all follow her lead.

As soon as we're clear of the earthen banks, we see the outline of figures moving in the distance. Frightened squeals rise up from the pig enclosures and bellowing from the cows as the silhouetted figures cry out to each other, realising we are out and quickly trying to move the animals out of the pens. Any attempt at keeping the animals quiet has been abandoned.

We ride swiftly as one, heading towards the nearest crossing point of the river Stiffkey. The crisp night air stings my eyes and nose as we pick up speed. I can feel Morna's tension and anxiety echo my own – what are we riding into?

At the river, we cross the planked walkway, Morna as solid and steady as ever. Any exhaustion she's feeling from our day's journey is replaced by adrenalin.

The sounds from the paddocks are becoming more

frantic. We rush towards them, our eyes peeled for signs of movement on any sides, our shields protecting ourselves and our horses as best we can. I feel lucky to be near the inside of the pack, my father to my right and another clan warrior to my left, an old family friend.

Brenna is just in front of me, with three other clan warriors leading the charge. Behind us more junior warriors are clustered, including my friends, and further behind them the experienced warriors shield the sides and rear. I can imagine this is a normal formation – the adults who have done this so many times before naturally taking their places without any discussion. At one time, they were the ones on the inside; now they are the protectors.

From this sheltered position, I can scan the distance and see what we're approaching. We've had to slow down our pace slightly as we ride over the bumpy land surrounding the riverbed; if a horse gets a hoof stuck, it could be down in a minute – and could pull others down around it as it falls. The action ahead seems chaotic, with shadowy figures moving every which way. My heart quickens as we draw near; I wonder if we're going to have to fight or if they'll abandon their raid.

Luckily, they don't seem able to organise the animals very quickly; there's still a huge amount of noise coming across and the sounds of scuffles.

Suddenly, Brenna speaks a loud, clear, 'Halt!' and the warriors in front draw up their horses, the rest of us behind following suit. We come to a standstill in a group and Brenna quickly calls out the order: 'Archers – ready your bows.'

This is me. My heart rises up to my throat as I quickly pull out my bow, loading an arrow. There are five of us now ready, aiming straight ahead. 'Aim long,' Brenna says, 'and land behind.'

'LOOSE,' she says, and we release simultaneously, the arrows arcing gracefully through the air and making their mark on the target area directly behind them – letting them know we have them pinned down.

The intruders seem confused, not sure which way to turn. Cries ring out, which startles the already frightened animals and creates more chaos as some of them try to run away.

'Again,' says Brenna, and we load the arrows again. 'And LOOSE,' she says. Once again we let go, and once again they fly straight and true.

Now we can see some figures gather off to the side of the paddocks, no longer so concerned with the animals but presumably trying to decide how to act in return.

Vastini once again blows the battle horn.

Brenna doesn't wait; she leads us on. 'Ready swords and shields,' she calls, '…and march!'

The raiding clan seems to hesitate, lowing their horses to and fro. We continue to ride on, straight towards them.

Just as I think this could be very bad, Brenna calls to

us again – 'Halt!' – and this time the response is almost instant. Our group of horses and warriors comes to a sudden stop just four rods away from the raiding clan. From this distance, I can see their bodies facing us, swords readied, faces painted in blue woad as warriors do when entering battle. I recognise the leader from the gates; it is the Hunstanton clan.

I prepare for Brenna to lead us in a charge; the warriors around me do the same, readying their swords and shields. She lifts her hand and suddenly there is total silence.

She calls out to the raiders: 'Hunstanton. It was wrong of us not to invite you, but that does not excuse this action. I could cut you down where you stand for trying to take what is ours. Or we could talk as equals. Which will it be?'

I am shocked to hear her talk so plainly, but fascinated to see the effect that it has; the surprised looks on the faces of the warriors around me tells me they feel the same way. Only my father remains unchanged, and I wonder if this is a familiar speech – or just a familiar Brenna.

The invaders mutter quickly amongst themselves, the tension mounting with every passing moment. I wonder, would I have charged? Would I have chosen this strategy?

A leader steps forward from the group and his answering voice finally calls out. 'Very well,' he relinquishes, 'we will talk. We'll return with our chief.'

A few moments pass with no action, and I wonder

if they'll change their minds and charge us instead. But then with a call of 'Away!,' they head off in the opposite direction – galloping west, back towards Hunstanton.

I hear a few whistles and calls around me as they start to clear the hill beyond; as the figures fade to sky, relief floods over me – they aren't coming back. I let out a deep sigh; it feels like I've been holding my breath since we left the hillfort. Brenna, now next to me, laughs.

'Exactly!' she says. 'Let's check the animals.'

When we reach the paddocks, we can see that most of the animals have settled back down, still in their paddocks. A few of the cows have set off up the hillside, but haven't gone any further; Drustan and two other junior warriors are able to round them up and get them back inside fairly quickly. They are spooked, but getting back into the security of their paddocks seems to settle them. They trot off towards the far side, hopefully back to sleep the rest of the night peacefully.

My father secures the paddocks and does one last check to make sure everything looks right. Then we gather together and Brenna splits us up: leaving some warriors to keep watch on the animals, others to stay in waiting for their turn back at the guard towers on the entrance gates, and the rest of us to return for a bit of sleep before daybreak.

Brenna herself remains on watch at the paddocks, seemingly reluctant to leave any of her clan at risk without her there as well. She smiles at me as I turn to go, and I think again of how she handled the situation in such a different way than I imagined.

Drustan and his horse fall in step beside Morna and I as we head back to the hillfort. 'Well,' he says, and gives a little laugh, 'that went better than expected!'

'Yes,' I agree. 'Thanks to Brenna,' I add.

'It was impressive,' he shakes his head incredulously. 'You have to hand it to her – she knows what she's doing.'

Yes, she does, I think to myself.

'You were amazing back there,' he adds, 'as always – straight on target and incredibly graceful.' I smile and feel my cheeks redden at the compliment.

We ride together, relieved to be going home.

THIRTEEN

When we arrive back at the hillfort, we're greeted by almost the entire clan – awake though it's the middle of the night. They had obviously done some quick work inside, gathering the people and letting them know things were okay, for now everyone stands clustered around the entrance gates, welcoming us back home.

Mam rushes over to me and sweeps me into her arms, showering my head with kisses, while Lucilia and Mato follow her in hugging my waist and legs. I laugh, slightly overwhelmed with the surge of love, but feel relieved to be home again in one piece.

With Brenna still out near the paddocks, my father takes charge and relays the events of the night, highlighting Brenna's strategic, diplomatic approach, and explaining the plan for tonight and tomorrow.

I hear murmurs arise here and there in the group;

obviously her decision is not without controversy.

'And now, my friends,' Bellator again addresses the assembled crowd. 'Let us try to get some sleep, for it will not be long before day breaks and we have much work to do. We must receive the Hunstanton clan as our guests, but must also be prepared in case things do not go as we hope.'

At this statement, the murmurs are no longer hushed and conversations break out all over. Some cries erupt from the crowd: 'But what about our children?' asks one. 'Why has Brenna put us in this situation?' asks another.

Bellator tries to hush them. 'My friends, my friends,' he says, his hands motioning quiet. 'It is no one's wish to enter battle, especially with fellow tribespeople. We must always try to resolve these matters without bloodshed. They are hurt; this is true. But we must try to talk with them, discuss the situation. They have agreed to this, and there is no reason to believe they will try to do us harm tomorrow. We mean only to be prepared, so as not to be taken unaware.'

Many people are still not happy about this. Senni and her family are near to us, also reunited with arms around each other's shoulders; she casts a worried look my way.

My father eventually succeeds in encouraging everyone back to bed, and the gathered crowd disperses towards their homes – although worried discussion continues to float back to my ears.

One of the last to go, Senni comes near. 'Do you think it will be okay?' she asks. 'Do you think people will go along with the plan?' I have an idea what she might be thinking – some of the clan could try to take matters into their own hands and revolt.

I consider this, but have to put my faith in Brenna.

'I think,' I say slowly, 'that I agree with my father and Brenna – we must always try to resolve our differences peacefully. And I think people will see it. I have to believe they will see it – that people are good at heart.'

I put my arm around my friend. 'But first,' I say jokingly, 'I think people need sleep.'

We both laugh, and she gives me a playful nudge. I rest my head on her shoulder.

'Thank you,' I say. 'Thank you for being there for me.'

'Always,' she says and gives me a tight hug. We part ways then, headed back to our own houses for a few hours of sleep.

The next morning comes cool and misty, as deeper autumn threatens to settle in. I wake early, despite the late night, and Mam sends me off immediately to fetch water from the river.

The hillfort is already alive with activity and preparations for the important meeting. Although there is excitement in the air, it is tinged with nervous anticipation. The fog hanging low over the roundhouses adds to the suspense and intrigue of the day. I shudder slightly involuntarily, but still feel comfortable in Brenna's decision; I just hope it goes as planned.

I hurry off through the gates and down to the river to complete my task, moving out of the fog as I come into the river valley. Immediately I feel better and laugh at myself for letting my imagination and senses carry me away.

On my way back to the fort, I come across Brenna also headed in that direction. She sees me and waves, looking bright and awake, though I wonder if she has even slept.

'Hello there, Cara. How are you this morning?' she asks.

'I am well, thank you,' I reply, 'but it's really I who should be asking you how you are.'

'Oh, the night was not too bad at all,' she replies.

'Are you just coming back from your watch?' I ask her.

'No,' she says, 'I've been back and forth a few times – just making sure everything is as it should be.'

She smiles and puts her arm around me as we walk. I struggle to hold the full basket of water in my hands but feel too honoured to receive her attention to pull away. 'You did very well last night,' she tells me earnestly. 'It's not easy to ride as part of a pack, nor to take commands, nor to shoot straight and true while feeling shaky with fear. Yet you did them all without hesitation.' I feel a wave of happiness rush over me.

'And how did you feel about my actions?' she asks. I consider the question carefully and answer truthfully.

'At first, I was very surprised, then a bit shocked and scared actually. Giving the other clan time to get away and the option to come back and take action against us – it didn't seem like the best thing to do. I wasn't the only one,' I rush on, 'lots of people were quite nervous, I think.'

She nods, knowingly. 'As they would be,' she says. 'People who are fearful often seek immediate action to dispel those fears. But this hasty course of action generally has worse, often unforeseen consequences. A physical response brings its own physical response, in time,' she adds.

I think about this. I can see her point, having heard tales of this throughout my short life. 'Is that why you wanted to talk then?' I ask her.

'Absolutely,' she says. 'There is always an answer; it's up to us to find it.'

We've reached the common area of the hillfort now and she releases me, then turns to go with a smile. She turns back – 'Do not be afraid, Carassouna. True bravery comes when we face our fears head on, with a clear mind and an open heart.' With that she is gone, into her roundhouse, to prepare for the meeting.

I head into my own house, warmed and heartened by

her words. I know she is the leader I want to be.

As the morning wears on the fog eventually lifts and you can almost hear a collective sigh of relief from the clan. Superstition can take hold on people in strange ways, and a clear, bright sky tends to make people feel more confident in a positive outcome.

The families of the clan have been working all morning to prepare for our visitors, to welcome them as guests while remaining on guard for any action. As they arrive, I can see many people bristled with fear and apprehension. Yet they stay silent, and Brenna remains as confident and welcoming as ever, smiling as she receives our guests and embracing the leaders as friends.

The leaders all file into the meeting house, where food and drink are served to welcome our guests. I am not invited in this time, but am not sad about that. On the contrary, I think back to my last experience and feel relieved I can just observe from the outside. I return to my roundhouse to help Mam prepare our lunch.

The afternoon wears on. At times, heated discussion can be heard from inside the meeting house, but after a while we hear laughter ring out. I'm playing with Mato outside when this happens, fashioning dolls out of sticks, straw and grass.

He loves his little dolls and pretends they need to fight in a great battle. 'But isn't it sad, Cara,' he says, 'that when people go to battle, they don't always come back? Where do they go?'

'Well, Mato, no one knows exactly,' I say to him gently. 'But you're right – it is very sad. And that's why Brenna is such a great leader,' I continue, 'she wants to make sure everyone comes back.'

He looks slightly puzzled, and I ruffle his hair. 'Don't you worry, little one, we're in good hands,' I say, thinking back to the last time someone told me that. He returns to his game, moving all of his dolls home to their beds to sleep. I think about the laughter I can hear – how very different that is from the sounds we may have heard last night had she chosen a different action.

Eventually the clan of Hunstanton leaves our hillfort. The leaders of both clans embrace each other in turn before they go, laughing and joking and generally in good cheer. Our clan gathers to wave them off, then our leaders call us together and tell us some of the meeting, and the result – which we all can guess – that both have gone away at peace.

'There were some compromises to be made,' Brenna says, 'of course – as there always must be in discussions. But things feel now as they should, and I think we have an ally once again.'

Cheers rise up from the group, and I feel a surge of happiness, relief and peace. The worries and concerns that have plagued my mind seem to be swept away, replaced by a sense of safety and security.

I feel tears fill my eyes as I'm overwhelmed by emotions, when suddenly Senni surprises me with a giant hug. I hadn't even seen her come up next to me. She kisses my cheek, and I laugh out loud.

Drustan approaches the two of us as we stand together, crying, laughing and hugging. 'Now I feel left out,' he says, and we take him into our fold. I've never been happier – loved by my two best friends, surrounded by my family and clan.

I enjoy the moment and try to savour these feelings. I know they can't last, given the secrets I know of Thornham. A little niggle in the back of my mind takes hold as I realise Hunstanton won't be an ally for long, if what we think is true.

'Do you know what I think we need?' asks Senni.

Drustan and I look at each other. He shrugs; I shake my head.

'A trip to the seaside,' she says.

'That sounds perfect,' I agree. 'I can't imagine anywhere more perfect we could go right now.'

'You think we'll be able to get permission for a journey?' Drustan asks. 'After everything that's happened?'

'Leave it to me,' I say. 'I think I have a plan.'

FOURTEEN

It wasn't too difficult to convince our parents to let us go to the seaside. Mam was excited about the possibility of some lichen to make a fuschia dye, and everyone loves samphire – it's a savoury, salty treat. We promise to bring back enough for all of our families. I think they know we could use a little break as well – as long as we're careful and watchful.

Just after breakfast, Senni arrives at my house, cheerful and upbeat. 'Good morning everyone!' she calls out, breezing through the open doorway. Outside the sun is shining bright, warming the chill air, and she seems to bring the sunshine right in with her, illuminating even the dark edges of the house.

My mother and father are still sitting at the table, sipping their morning drinks, and return her cheerful greeting. Mato is threading beads on a string, while Lucilia is helping me prepare a picnic; they both stop what they are doing to rush over with a hug for Senni, almost knocking her down in their enthusiasm. Eventually she untangles herself and makes it over to me.

'It is a happy day,' I say to her and hug her with one arm, the other messy from preparing food. She kisses me on the cheek and ruffles my hair; still my big sister at heart.

Then she bends down and picks up Mato, holding him on her hip so he can see the table.

'Look at this glorious picnic, Senni,' Lucilia says excitedly. 'Cows cheese and goats cheese, freshly baked rosemary and garlic bread, blackberry cake and even honey tea in a flask.'

'Mm, that looks amazing – and smells amazing!' Senni says appreciatively.

'Let me wash up,' I say, 'then I'll be ready to go.' I head outside to clean my hands in the water bucket by the side of the house, then return to my sleeping area to get changed for our journey ahead. As I'm pulling my dress over my head, I hear a rustle and turn around in surprise. Mam has snuck in.

'I'm sorry, Cara,' she says very quietly, 'I didn't mean to startle you. I just wanted a word with you alone.'

'Oh?' I ask.

'I just wanted to tell you…' she looks quite choked up now, almost close to tears.

'What is it, Mam?' I ask worriedly.

She can't get the words out before the tears come. 'I'm just so proud of you, Cara,' she says through her tears, brushing them away hurriedly.

'Oh, Mam,' I say, throwing my arms around her. I sometimes forget my mother is at heart such a gentle person, quite sensitive. She's so stoic for the rest of us.

She pulls back and looks at me lovingly, brushing my hair away from my face.

'I know about Drustan as well,' she says quietly.

I gasp, shocked – how could she know? I don't even know what I feel!

She rests her hands on my shoulders, her eyes dancing. 'Don't be so surprised, my dear, I was young once too,' she says. 'I see the way you look at each other, especially when the other isn't looking. Young love.'

I blush embarrassedly. Then start to worry. 'Does Tad know?' I whisper urgently.

She shakes her head, smiling a bit sadly. 'Not yet, I don't think,' she says. 'And I won't tell him…yet.'

'Ultimately you have to do what is right for you, Cara, I believe that. And your father believes that. But remember, you are not you alone – your clan is part of you as well, and you have to consider the impact on others…if only because of the effect it will have on your life.'

'But for now,' she kisses me on the forehead then looks straight into my eyes, 'be happy.' She turns and leaves, as quietly as she came, leaving me slightly stunned behind.

I can hear the voices of the others in the main part of the roundhouse; I don't think they heard our hushed conversation. I hope not. As I leave my sleeping area, no one looks at me strangely or accusingly – I don't think they heard.

'Well,' I say, somewhat forcing cheerfulness, 'shall we go, Senni?'

'Definitely,' she replies, 'it's a very long walk. And Drustan will be waiting for us.'

My mother looks at me meaningfully and I feel myself blush in her gaze.

Luckily Tad saves me from myself and comes over to give me a giant hug, scooping me up off the ground as he always did when I was little.

'You've done well, Cara,' he says a bit gruffly, 'and you deserve some fun.' He squeezes me a little tighter, then sets me down again. 'Just make sure you come home again,' he says, mostly playfully but with a hint of seriousness.

'And don't forget my lichen,' Mam adds. 'The darker orange the better; and not too dry.'

'Of course, Mam,' I say, secretly rolling my eyes in Senni's direction. Although I'm excited too – a new colour for our clothes.

We gather our things and leave the roundhouse, waving to my family as they stand in the doorway sending us off for the day. Making this kind of journey is a major undertaking – with most of the day spent travelling, there are so many things that could happen.

We walk around the meeting house, my family now hidden from view, and come across Drustan waiting for us at the doorway, leaning against a post. He looks very relaxed, and – I can't help it – very handsome. My heart does a little flip flop, and I think of my mother's words, 'For now, be happy.' I smile at him warmly and he returns my smile. I can feel myself beaming, my cheeks flushed, and Senni looks at us strangely.

'Let's set off,' I say quickly, trying to brush it off.

Once the hillfort is out of sight, we fall into a contented silence as we walk – happy in each other's company, happy for the sunshine to warm the cool air, happy for the peace and birdsong as we walk. I think back to our goodbyes at my house this morning, and wonder at my parents. It's as though each of them can see into my heart in different ways. My mother sees my heart's true love; my father its longing for adventure.

We walk up and down gentle hills covered in grass and wildflowers, roughly following the river Stiffkey as it winds its way towards the sea. Senni is the leader, having taken advice on how best to reach the point she wants to take us to. None of us have ever been there before, and it's exciting venturing out on our own, exploring together.

As we reach the salt marshes, we head east, away from the river, walking parallel to the sea although we often lose sight of it. We're lucky the sun is out today, or I wonder how we would find our way home again. The salt marshes are a vast, desolate expanse, almost buried at high tide while greatly exposed at low – with the sea feeling deceptively close. Once you get out past the treeline, the land appears flat all the way to the horizon, covered in green and brown brush. But hidden pools and muddy creeks wind their way throughout, sometimes almost invisible until you stumble upon them. The mud pulls you in, sucks you down, until you feel you might be stuck there forever. With no real landmarks, it's easy to get disoriented and walk the wrong way – and even get stuck out at sea as the water comes in.

Luckily, Senni has heard of a point, sheltered from the wind by sand dunes and always out of water. After almost a league, we turn north, heading northeast, and soon the sea comes fully into sight. As we walk towards it, I am at once reminded how small and insignificant I am, how minor my troubles actually are. All of this – as far as you can see on the horizon – and who knows what lies beyond?

We arrive at the seaside as the tide is going out and Senni shows us the firm sandy path stretching straight out ahead, leading to the spot she wants to take us.

'Should we collect the lichen and samphire first?' I ask.

'Let's pick as we go,' she says, 'there should be plenty on our way.'

As we walk, I am at once struck by the peace and solitude of this place. Sheltered from the mainland on one side by sandy dunes, the immense sea forms the other side – the sandy walkway in between. Senni tells us that this sand is buried in low tide, and then you have to walk out on shingle; much harder going than the sand. We pass mysterious fishing birds – Senni calls them oystercatchers – and see terns and other seabirds resting up in the brush of the dunes.

After walking another league down this point, Senni seems satisfied that we've reached the final spot, nestled against a dune for protection. We take off our cloaks and lay them down together, putting our bags on top to keep them from blowing away, then take off our shoes and sit down. I love to put my feet in the sand and feel the grains between my toes.

I set my hand down on top of a shell and remember the shell still safe within my pouch. I take it out and admire the beautiful curve and colour of this shell I collected the last time I was at the sea; before I knew this was all called sand.

Senni breaks into my reverie, stands up again for a moment. 'Cara, there's something I want you to see.'

I stand up and follow her, climbing the dune behind her and Drustan. As we reach the top, I realise how much shelter the dunes provide; the cool, brisk air suddenly whips my hair against my face, stinging my eyes and darting into my mouth. I pull it back with one hand and look to where Senni is pointing, some hundred feet away.

There, rolling on the sand, is a herd of large, grey animals – seals. I've only ever seen a seal once before, but Drustan is very familiar with them; he tells us they also live in herds on the coast near his fosterage. For me, they seem otherworldly.

We stand and watch them until we start shivering in the cold air, then climb back down to our little space below.

The seashell still in my hand, I sit back down in awe of this magical place.

'What do you have there?' Drustan asks.

I show him the shell. I give a little shudder as my mind drifts to how uncertain everything still is for our clan – more than my friends know. Drustan, thinking I'm cold, takes off his tunic and puts it over my shoulders.

'Thank you,' I say to him, and he smiles in return.

Senni is busy unpacking the picnics, laying them out on the blanket before us.

'What a feast!' Drustan exclaims. 'I'm famished.'

We all dig in to the food, hungry and tired after our long journey here.

Senni is the first one to break the silence of hungry people eating. 'I've missed this,' she says. 'Just breathe in the air.' I take a deep breath. 'Can you feel how it's different?' she asks. 'Salty, fresh, alive.'

'And wet,' I add. We both laugh. The moist air does

feel good, and fresh. I feel more alive with each breath.

'The sound of the waves lapping the shore,' she continues, looking out across the water as she speaks. 'The feeling of movement when the waves gently rock against your ankles and legs, or against your boat when you're out at sea.'

We are all silent then, watching the waves roll in and staring across the vast water to the horizon.

'I just feel this connection,' Senni finally continues, 'at one with the waves, the sea, everything. It's so peaceful. It makes me feel like everything is going to be okay.' She laughs. 'Although I suppose that's a bit silly,' she says.

'No, it's not,' I tell her. 'I can understand what you mean, why you feel that way. Especially as you've spent so much time there now, right by the sea.'

'Yes,' she says, 'the Thornham clan is pretty much as close to the sea as you can get. We even fish straight from the estuary. And you wouldn't believe some of the dyes they can make! They experiment with all the lichen on the beach – my favourite is purple, the colour of lavender. I intend to make my best dress in that colour as soon as I can,' she adds.

'I would love it,' I say, 'anything but blue.'

We both laugh, knowing my mam's funny quirks.

'I wonder why they didn't come?' Senni suddenly asks, almost to herself.

'Who? Where?' I say. 'Here?'

'No,' Senni says, 'sorry. I was thinking aloud…I just wonder why the clan of Thornham didn't come to the tribal meeting. I'm pretty sure they were invited…'

I stay silent, not sure what to say to her.

'But, you know,' she continues, 'they haven't made any demands. I mean, Hunstanton made it clear pretty quickly that they were upset about not being invited…do you think they could have just forgotten? Or something happened…do you think they're okay?'

This thought, suddenly just occurring, seems to set her into a panic.

I try to soothe her, 'Senni, I'm sure they are fine. We would have heard if something was truly wrong – we always get news through.'

She looks somewhat appeased, but not fully.

'Today's not the day,' I say to her. 'There's nothing we can do right now. Just remember how much you loved it there.' I can see her trying to get her mind back there. 'The peace, the serenity…' I say, '…the sea, the boats. It all sounds wonderful,' I add.

'It really was,' she says, looking back out to sea and smiling again. 'I can remember now,' she adds, 'how much I loved the boats – I often went out on the fishing trips; there are very different fish that live in the sea to the rivers and estuaries.'

As she sinks into her own reverie, I think this is a good time for Drustan to finally tell us about his time away –

and why he doesn't want to talk about it.

I break the silence by saying, 'So what about you, Drustan? Will you finally tell me about yours?'

He looks away, not meeting my gaze.

I try again. 'It was in a hillfort, right? At Caistor St Edmund? I've heard that's very busy…what was it like?'

'Okay,' he says reluctantly, brushing his hands off and turning to face us both. 'If you insist,' he says with a sigh.

'Yes, it's busy. It's one of the main ports coming in from the sea so it has travellers pretty much constantly passing through, and goods from other lands, and animals, that sort of thing. People float down the river Yare in longboats from the sea, or they arrive on foot travelling from the Catuvellauni or Trinovantes lands. The hillfort has three huge meeting houses to receive all the travellers! They also use these as sleeping areas for people stopping over. There's always so much going on.' He seems caught up in the memory of his experience now.

'Did you enjoy the busyness? What was it like?' I ask.

He laughs, 'Some of the time. Sometimes it felt really exciting and like I could go anywhere or do anything. It wouldn't be hard – just get in with a group headed back out to their boat or take up trading and head inland.'

'My foster family was huge,' he continues. 'Ten children, most of them girls. It wasn't so bad at first; it was kind of nice, actually – always having someone you could talk to, someone to work with, sing songs with, dance with...'

'But the last year I was there – once I turned eleven – well, that was completely different. They had three daughters just a bit older than me, and they all seemed to think I was "meant" for them. They wouldn't leave me alone! You know how I hate to be the centre of attention.' He shakes his head in frustration and I nod knowingly. That is pretty much Drustan's worst nightmare – he would much rather just fade into the background, be part of the group.

He sighs and continues, 'Maybe that's why their parents had taken in a boy? I don't know. I kept telling them I wasn't interested, but they didn't seem to think it was possible. They were horrible to each other, and it was horrible to watch. I was just ready to leave. I wanted so badly to get out of there! It was pretty hard sometimes not to just run away with some group of travellers – ANY group of travellers!' Drustan laughs, and Senni and I join in, glad he can make light of the situation now.

'That does sound tense,' I sympathise. 'I'm sorry you had to go through that. I can imagine you hated that attention, especially feeling like you were in the way.'

'Mmhmm,' he nods emphatically.

'So why didn't you leave?' I ask him. 'How did you manage to hang on until it was time to come back? It sounds like you could have gone anywhere! Such a thrilling thought,' I add enviously.

Drustan looks me straight in the eye. 'Because of you,' he says. My heart feels as though it stops, then pounds out of my chest. Can he hear it?

'I knew you were meant to marry Gavo…and I was worried you might be happy about that. I just had no idea,' he says frankly. 'I hoped one day I might be able to tell you how I feel – but I didn't know if it would ever be possible.'

He smiles, 'When you told me you weren't sure of your choice, it meant I had a chance.'

I'm silent while he says all of this, holding my breath. Now I let it out, overwhelmed at this news but happy.

I find myself looking at him in a new light. I know I care for him too. Time seems to stand still as I hear the waves gently lapping at the shore and feel the warm sun on my face.

Senni breaks the moment, sitting up and pouring tea for us from a carrying pouch into small clay cups. She lifts her cup to toast and we follow suit.

'To good friends,' she says, 'and to new possibilities,' she adds, looking at us both with a smile. We tap cups and drink the refreshing honey tea.

When I finish, I tuck my seashell back in my pouch, safe and sound for whenever I need it – now as a reminder of happiness and peace.

'Do you think we've done enough for the day?' Senni asks finally.

'There's always time for more adventure, Senni, you know that,' I say, smiling mischievously.

But we must leave – there's just enough daylight left to reach home. Drustan starts to pack up our picnic and we all join in, then brush the sand off our cloaks.

After one last long look out to sea, we turn and head back towards home, the tide slowly creeping in as we go.

Back on the mainland, we set off west. Drustan walks close to me as the sun starts to make its way down the horizon, so close I can feel the warmth emanating from him and it seems he is an extension of the sun. Senni chatters away as we walk, making conversation enough for all of us.

I'm happy to be left with my thoughts as they somersault through my head – the secret door, the hidden path; worried thoughts for Senni and new feelings for Drustan. And what do I want? To set off and explore? To stay home and train to lead?

There are so many decisions to make, so many changes to come. Samhain is approaching now, and with it the new year. Soon the travelling group will set off on its dangerous mission, but first I must tell Brenna what I have found. Even if I get in serious trouble for going out on my own, she needs to know.

My fate may lie in leaving home, but I will do my best to protect it and all those people I love so dearly while I am here. For I am home.

Acknowledgements

To my family, and especially Brian:
Thank you for putting up with my 'project'
for so many years and traipsing around
Britain to visit sites and museums.

Thank you to all of my family and friends:
I am grateful every day for your love and support.

Thank you to Izzie for being my first test reader, and
to all of my test readers: Emily, Katherine, Paige,
Maddy and Libby. Thank you especially to Josephine
whose feedback was essential to the story.

And to the many Iron Age historians and researchers:
Thank you for striving to understand this amazing time
period despite the lack of written records -
and for making this information available for
everyone to access.
I hope you enjoy this book.

WILL THE CATUVELLAUNI ATTACK?

ARE THORNHAM AND HUNSTANTON
SECRETLY MEETING?

WILL CARA CHOOSE DRUSTAN?

ANSWERS TO ALL THIS
AND MORE IN THE NEXT

CARASSOUNA
BOOK

COMING AUTUMN
2019 AD

VISIT
WWW.CARASSOUNA.COM

Made in the USA
Middletown, DE
09 November 2018